POOR FARM

a novel

RONAN O'DRISCOLL

Cover image: Rebekah Wetmore
Author photo: Niki Davison, Snickerdoodle Photography
(snickerdoodle.ca)
Editor: Andrew Wetmore

ISBN: 978-1-7772937-8-9
First edition April, 2021

MOOSE HOUSE
PUBLICATIONS

397 Parker Mountain Road
Granville Ferry NS
B0S 1A0
moosehousepress.com
info@moosehousepress.com

We live and work in Mi'kma'ki, the ancestral and unceded territory of the Mi'kmaq People. This territory is covered by the "Treaties of Peace and Friendship" which Mi'kmaq and Wolastoqiyik (Maliseet) People first signed with the British Crown in 1725. The treaties did not deal with surrender of lands and resources but in fact recognized Mi'kmaq and Wolastoqiyik (Maliseet) title and established the rules for what was to be an ongoing relationship between nations. We are all Treaty people.

Poor Farm is a work of historical fiction. Apart from the well-known actual people, events and locales that figure in the narrative, all names, characters, places and incidents are the products of the author's imagination or are used fictitiously. Any resemblance to current events or living persons is entirely coincidental.

Visit https://poor.farm for supplemental background material.

The song fragment beginning "Horo hi rithill" is from *MacEdward Leach and the Songs of Eastern Canada.* A version is available at
www.mun.ca/folklore/leach/songs/CB/3-03.htm

"The Silvery Tide" and "Go and Tell Aunt Nabbie" are from Helen Creighton, *Traditional Songs from Nova Scotia.*

Sometimes I actually pity you for not being able to see the beauty of the world in the same way we do. Really, our vision of the world can be incredible, just incredible.

Naoki Higashida

I perched for rest and imagined
cuckoos calling across water,
the Bann cuckoo, calling sweeter
than church bells that whinge and grind.

Friday is the wrong day, woman,
for you to give birth to a son,
the day when Mad Sweeney fasts
for love of God, in penitence.

From *Sweeney Astray* by Seamus Heaney

To Martin
Still Learning

Contents

Tims

Cole Harbour, Nova Scotia, one hundred and thirty years later

I'm Tim.

We moved to Cole Harbour a few years ago. It's not that different from Ireland: the strip malls are uglier, the roads better. A sign on the way into town says "Birthplace of Sidney Crosby". Was he a politician from history? Turns out he's a hockey star.

I drove past the sign into the countryside spotted with melting snow. Pausing at a stop sign, I watched a few big flakes drift onto the car windscreen—geometric shapes spidering down from the dull sky. They appeared insect-like on the glass before dissolving.

I'm still not used to all the snow. That and forests everywhere. You don't have that in Ireland—these great blank tracts of trees. It would be all farms and houses back home.

"Ah, aaah. Aaah. Ah."

Daniel broke my reverie from the back seat. I realized I was pausing too long at the empty crossroads. We were alone.

"Y'alright there, Daniel?" I asked, easing the car forward.

No reply.

"Want me to put on some music?"

Silence.

Not too long ago, we couldn't drive anywhere without crappy pop music blaring on the radio. One day, for no obvious reason, he started screaming every time music came on, even the jingle for the news. Now, he might tolerate a CD.

I let the silence resume rather than fumbling around for a disc. We're nearly there, anyway.

Daniel is eight and autistic. I suppose there are fancier ways of putting it. Once I said it to someone at my office. His response surprised me.

"Yeah? But how autistic?"

There was a nasty edge to his voice—the tone reserved for annoyance about vegans, gluten intolerance, scent sensitivity or whatever. I stared at him, frozen. After a shocked pause, I murmured, "Autistic enough..."

I never brought the topic up again.

"You're not going to fucking Tims," Daniel announced from the back seat.

This phrase you can say? I growled it once to my other kids, and they roared with laughter as Daniel mimicked me perfectly. We had praised him. According to the therapists, we should reward all speech effort. It stopped being funny after he kept repeating it. Whenever he said "you", he meant himself.

"No. Not going to Tims," I agreed, spotting a Tims billboard in the rear view mirror. Tims are everywhere here —the Canadian equivalent of pubs. Oh, there are bars, but everyone meets at Tims. As a Tim, it bothered me there was no apostrophe in the name.

Woodlots and fields lined Bissett Road as the houses thinned out. Soon we neared another Cole Harbour landmark: the trailer park where they filmed the *Trailer Park Boys*. This had no official sign, but my mother-in-law pointed it out to me early on. When we told friends we were moving to Canada, they had asked, "Nova Scotia? Isn't that where the Trailer Park Boys are from?"

I have heard that, like Sidney Crosby, Bubbles and the other trailer park boys live in much grander, more exclusive parts of HRM. They are Halifax royalty and you wouldn't expect them to live in trailer parks.

HRM doesn't stand for Her Royal Majesty but for Halifax Regional Municipality. My father, on his first visit, had made this mistake when he saw HRM signs everywhere. He had lived in London, so he thought the signs meant the Queen. He liked Canada, though, and considered everything bigger, and by extension, better.

Cole Harbour is a suburb of this giant, under-populated city.

"Fine sized house," Dad had said with approval. "Better than that over-priced shed ye had in Dublin."

Daniel puzzled him, even when a toddler. Why did he not smile or even look at you? Wasn't he awful late in talking? Funny, Dad was the first to notice the signs. Once we knew about autism, we realized it was common on my side of the family.

The trail entrance was across the road from the empty trailer park. I pulled into the parking lot, past the sign.

Cole Harbour Nature Trail

"Here we are, Daniel. Let's go for a walk. Daddy has a picnic for us."

"You want walk."

He loves to go for a walk. Although it's hard to know what he means when he echoes what you say. Is he saying something or parroting to appease your need for conversation? It's called echolalia.

Our boots made a crunching sound as we walked along the snow-covered trail—the babbling of running water everywhere under the canopy of tall trees. The spring melt swelled the little brook alongside the path.

As we walked, Daniel pulled and batted at any vegetation starting to sprout by the trail side. Sometimes he hummed tunelessly. Other times he became agitated and repeatedly hit a bush or low branch. I always hurry him along when this happens.

Joggers and dog walkers pretended not to observe his strange behaviour. People are usually very circumspect here: don't have to interfere if you don't see. Another similarity to Ireland.

We came to a park bench, not as mildewed as some and mostly dry.

"Why don't we eat here, Daniel? You sit down and I'll get our snacks out of the bag."

No reply as he sat down. I fumbled with the backpack. Let's try healthy stuff first.

"How about an orange?"

I put the orange down before sitting beside him. *Crap.* The bench was wetter than I thought.

"No orange."

OK. Two-word replies are good. With food, his communication is at its best.

"No? How about a cheese-string, then?"

Cheese-strings were processed food, but he devoured the things. Usually. There were only a few items he reliably ate, and I was running out of options.

"No cheese."

"Well, Daniel. Eat something. Here's Daddy's snack."

I placed a tray of supermarket sushi between us.

"Let's see what else is in the bag."

I was rummaging around in the bag so only caught him pushing my lunch off the bench out of the corner of my eye. The food landed face-down in the black, water-logged soil.

"Jesus Christ," I exploded. "Daniel! That was my lunch. What's Daddy going to eat now?"

I grabbed him by the shoulders, joggling him. He glanced at me before looking away, beautiful face impass-ive. His eyelashes were long and dark, like a girl's.

"Aw, Daniel," I shouted in frustration, quickly letting go of him. I hated this, losing my temper. It didn't help that he had woken at two that morning and it took my wife an hour to get him back to sleep as he screamed and laughed. Taking him for a walk outdoors today was a bid to tire him out in hopes of a decent sleep tonight.

"That's it," I growled. "No picnic."

I swept whatever I could salvage into the bag. Then I picked the remains of my lunch out of the dirt, depositing it in a nearby rusty barrel functioning as a rubbish bin.

"Come on," I said.

I jerked him up by his hand and got him walking along the trail. He followed along, making no sound.

I stewed in anger as we walked. *Why me?* His condition affected my entire life: marriage, job, everything. He was my mute jailer in this lifelong prison sentence. I couldn't look at him, I was so angry.

"Come *on*," I stressed when he lagged a little. "This way."

We walked past a strange clearing in the woods. We were on an unfamiliar trail without signs. In my agitation, I had taken an unusual route.

"I'm not saying it again. You'd better stay close."

The anger was peaking now, although I nursed it by dwelling further on my misfortune.

An image came unbidden to my mind: I remembered the temper my father could get into. I would giddily try not to laugh as his eyes bulged and nostrils flared. One time, I left the cutlery drawer open by mistake while Dad crouched underneath, fishing for something. He stood up, catching his head on the edge of the drawer. He cursed violently and looked at me, real murder in his eyes. I could only stare at his transfigured features, caught in the path of a stampeding bull. Thank god my mother didn't keep sharp knives in that drawer.

His anger never lasted, though, and Dad has mellowed a lot with age.

"Come over here now," I commanded.

There was a bend in the path and I led him along it. Past the bend, the trail broadened to a clearing. I noticed yellow grass peeking through the snow—not the usual gravel trail. At the far end was a stand of silver birch. Beyond the trees, I could make out the sea.

Dotted between the trees were about twenty wooden crosses. No names announced who was buried there, just simple two-by-fours painted white.

"What's this?" I asked as we wandered up to the graves.

Daniel started pulling at saplings growing amongst the crosses. I wandered about, mouth open, feeling cold all over. A bitter wind swept in from the broad bay beyond the trees.

The ground was uneven and broken, flagstones sticking out from the patchy snow. I wondered if they were headstones marking graves or the ruins of a building.

"Let's get out of here," I murmured. I directed Daniel back out to the main trail.

Who was buried back there? When had it happened? The crosses looked relatively new. Why was there no sign explaining the grim scene? Although we had visited the area before, I'd never taken much notice of the signs on the way in. All I could recall was that the entire area used to be a farm, donated to the encroaching city decades ago.

"You want orange," Daniel said, not looking at me.

"What? Oh. Right."

The trail opened onto an extensive field, part of the original farm, I supposed. The view out over the broad salt marsh estuary was stirring, even on a grey March Sunday. Pine forest dotted the distant shore. An osprey floated aloft. There was a strange bush with red leaves fluttering in the breeze. I wondered at it. Shouldn't the leaves have fallen off months ago?

Nearby was another bench.

"Sit down here," I said, my voice calmer now.

He sat, staring out over the water.

I fished an orange from the bag, piercing the tough skin with my thumb.

Then I started crying.

"I'm so sorry, Daniel," I said as best I could. "Sometimes it gets so hard with you. Do you see what I mean? I'm trying to do my best but I don't think it's enough. I love you, I really do. But it's so hard."

I sobbed like a child. *Christ*, what if someone we knew saw me? Hardly anyone here knew me, and *that* was my concern?

Futilely, I wiped my eyes with the back of my glove. I imagined I heard someone sniggering at the foolishness of trying to communicate with this child. I made a noise of anguish, recalling how rough I had been with him earlier. He was the gentlest soul I knew, and I treated him like that. My cheeks burned with tears.

"You want orange."

I blinked twice. He was looking at me without expression, head cocked to one side.

"Right. Orange."

I swallowed and took a deep breath, shudders of sobs subsiding. Blinking some more, I fumbled with the orange. I find crying akin to vomiting. You often feel better afterwards. I suppose the body compensates for the trauma by flooding itself with hormones.

I also realized how hungry I was. As I fed him the little orange, I calmed down enough to weigh my options.

"There's that McDonalds on Main Street. Want to get a burger there?"

It was worth a try, although he hated the noise, especially the canned music. Plus, I hated feeding him that crap all the time.

No reply. That meant yes.

"OK. Let's go, so."

We trudged back through the snow. It was tough going along the steep hill, but it was the quickest way back. Daniel stopped often, pondering nothing.

I was so self-absorbed, I nearly missed the sign.

The Halifax County Poor's Farm (1887-1929)
You are looking out over the fields and site of the Halifax County Poor's Farm (or Poor Farm) towards the Cole Harbour Salt Marsh...

It rambled a bit, as historical signs do. I scanned ahead, noting the grim black and white portraits of a superintendent and matron. Another dim photo showed vague forms penned in by a cluster of buildings.

One sentence jumped out at me:

By 1890, five major buildings and support buildings were housing up to 80 "inmates" that included "paupers" and the "harmlessly insane."

That would explain the unmarked graves.

"There might have been someone like you, Daniel," I said.

He was picking at the snow, putting it in his mouth.

"Shit. Don't eat that. All right, we're going."

My mind raced as we walked up to the car. Half paying attention, I scanned another historical sign by the car park, pondering the details.

How were autistics treated in the past? I had hardly heard of autism before the doctor had mumbled the word. She recommended we research the topic for ourselves. Her tone was limp, and she hardly looked at us. I stumbled out a question about a cure and treatment. She gave me a shocked look, as if I had mentioned faith-healing. Then she stood up to find disability tax credit forms.

If a fully-educated modern doctor had no clue what to do about autism, what had it been like before? History must be full of people like Daniel—mutes and the "harmlessly insane". Were they treated like animals? Or worse? Were they given up by their families to grim institutions like the one in that picture?

The farm burned down in 1929, the ruins bulldozed in the fifties. All that survived were two dozen anonymous wooden crosses a local historical society erected. Nobody knew exactly how many were buried in the mass grave.

I don't believe in ghosts. In fact, I try my best not to believe in anything. But standing by the perspexed sign in that muddy parking lot, I felt something. A memory lingering here: a story to be told, long forgotten.

I finally noticed Daniel whacking his glove on the side of the car. His grey sweatpants were stained dark with his piss. Everything made sense. I had forgotten to take him to the toilet before we left. He must have been wet and cold the whole time I bullied and blubbered about. The hunger in my gut turned sour.

"Oh, Daniel! I'm so sorry...I really am."

No more tears of self-pity. Just guilt. I took off my coat and laid it on the back seat for him.

"Here. Sit on this. We'll go to the drive-thru for burgers and eat them at home. There'll be no music there."

The winter wind whipped off the estuary and straight through me as I walked around to my side of the car.

Stained glass

St. Patrick's Catholic Church, Brunswick Street, Halifax, July 1875

Your first memory was the stained-glass window. It was in the church where the family went to mass. You always sat near it, in the last seats at the back. In the glass, a main figure crouched down under a heavy broken chair, wearing a wooden crown on his head. Around the crown was a yellow circle. Figures in the background, without wooden crowns, whipped this man. There was no sound in the scene. Frozen in the glass, all the noise of the world happened outside. The man could say nothing about how heavy the wood on his back or head was. The men with whips, also trapped in the window, didn't care.

Once, something beautiful happened—light shone through. The whole side of the pew filled with a shattered rainbow and the pain of not being heard, of not even being able to speak, eased for the stained-glass man. Speckles of colour settled on the faces of the family: the mother, the father, the brothers and sisters, even you. This beauty was so intense, your chest filled with a feeling you had to release.

You made joyful sounds to turn the beautiful light into music. The faces twisted in their strange ways—eyebrows turning towards each other and lips pressed together. The rest of the church, even the important man at the front in the long robes, went silent. You were even happier then.

Ronan O'Driscoll

Your next memory was being pulled out of the church by your father and having to leave the beautiful light, kicking and pulling to get back. Funny how a blow to the ear doesn't hurt at first: the ringing in the head takes over and distracts from the later pain.

The true sorrow was the memory—that first memory —of the figure trapped in the coloured glass escaping. In a church filled with people, the beauty of the escape of the man in pain went unobserved except by you. And they beat you for it.

There are other memories, and they have an order. Memories must be lined up properly to make sense. No matter how little sense things make, memories can make a story.

For example, the family never took you to church again. There was no memory of going there again. So you will never see those windows with the stained glass again.

As a child, when you were left alone, there was the problem of the cheese. Cheese is a favourite. A favourite means it takes over from everything else. A favourite is like the light shining through the stained glass. Anyway, cheese is a favourite.

The family had gone, but the cheese was in the kitchen, in the high press. There was a yellow wheel up there. You had to pull a chair up to the cupboard to get to it. This was not a problem as nobody was there to stop you.

Reaching for the cheese, high in the press, you touched the soft surface. The potent smell was there, but you put the smell away for later. It was just enough to deal with the touch. All was going well until the excitement started. This is the part of the memory when the problems began.

You are not sure how the chair collapsed. The excitement, perhaps? The chair, cheese and you came down hard onto the floor. Pain bloomed like getting that blow on the head from father.

Why was there blood? Curious how the thick red mixed in with the pale yellow of the cheese. For a long time, you played with the sensation of it. Just the cheese in the fingers, cool and pliant. The pain forgotten because cheese is your favourite. In the memory, there was a beautiful part of having all that cheese to touch and play with.

You ate some of it. Sometimes, things eaten have to be brought back up by burping them out of your throat. This is a wetter kind of cheese but is also nice to touch, although not such a favourite.

You were startled by their shouting, the kitchen full with the returned family. Mother was holding her hands. "Oh, Jesus! He's got into the cheddar and destroyed the kitchen."

The brothers and sisters were yelling too, but the memory starts to fade at this point. The last you remember is the father hitting you again and locking you in a room without food.

Squire

An aged man, of a rather simple turn of mind, belonging to the same District, who had been working somewhere in the city for his food and clothing (but had very little of the latter), left the city and arrived sometime during the night at about a mile from the settlement; the night being very cold, got to work and made himself a camp with the boughs of trees, having no other instrument to do so with, but a jack-knife. He remained there for three or four days, until he was found by a good Samaritan who took him to his own house and washed his clothing with his own hands, as he was in a very unclean condition. As soon as the Overseers learned of the condition of the poor man, they immediately endeavoured to find a place for him, but failed.[...]

We merely cite this instance to show how much easier it would have been, if such an institution as a good Poor Farm was in operation, where this poor man could have been taken to, and where all the Poor of each District could be provided for, and where every resident capable of doing some kind of work could be employed. Your Committee there are of the opinion that if such an institution was procured for this County and properly managed, it would, in a great measure relieve the ratepayers of much of the present expenses, and would also be the means of cheering the spirits of the very depressed and suffering Poor.

Committee on the Poor Report,
presented January 1886
to the Halifax County Council

Harriet Roche squinted out at the blanket of fresh snow. She rubbed her chapped lips together, considering the scene beyond the front door.

"Close the door, mother," Regina called. "You'll catch your death."

The cold was bracing, but not unwelcome. Until last year, she would gladly head out in it: helping her husband Michael, checking livestock or clearing the odd gap burdened by fresh snow.

She grimaced at the memory. Forty years together before Michael died. He had left her the farm. She knew it was as much hers as his. Their daughters weren't too happy about it though, having other plans for the land.

She had held them off until this weakness. The fool of a doctor said it was a heart attack. Harriet wasn't sure. What kind of doctor was he? Always making obscure jokes, like some kind of jester. What did he know? Anyway, it was a weakness.

Now Regina was leaving. Going into the city to marry some accountant, both urging her to sell the land.

"Mother? Won't you come in?"

She kept her lips pursed for a long while, staring out. A distant osprey wheeled over the harbour. *Their* harbour.

"I'm donating it."

"What?" asked Regina. "Whatever do you mean?"

"The farm. County Overseer came by the other day. Wants to put a poor farm out here."

"What? We can't talk about this now. Come back to bed!"

There was irritation in Regina's voice. Like storm clouds over the estuary, Harriet sensed the coming argument. She relished it. Go out with a bang. She hated this lingering. This weakness.

"I've decided. I'm leaving it for the city to build a charitable institution. I will come and live with you and Edgar."

She smiled at her daughter's thunder-struck features. A sudden catch in her chest spoiled the feeling of victory.

"I had best lie down," she added, closing the door. "Bring my breakfast upstairs."

~

John George Bissett gave the reins a sharp pull. His pony came to an obedient stop in front of the Roche farmhouse, although she had to step forward as the momentum of the sleigh pushed her. Bissett, known as 'The Squire' because of his extensive land-holdings, looked around the ill-kept farmyard with disdain. The house was missing shingles and the roof, under a blanket of snow, bowed. He dismissed the dishevelled hen-house and snow-covered woodpile with a contemptuous glance.

He stepped down from his box-seat, taking care not to slide on the ice covering the yard. George wore a fine coon skin coat, the best for warmth. He wore his greying beard in the Shenandoah style, which added to the grimness of his tightly pursed mouth. His eyes were intense and set deep in his face.

"Oh!" Regina called from the door. "Welcome, Mr. Bissett. Mind yourself out there. If you want to lead your horse up here, I'll fetch you a bucket of water."

Squire Bissett had a tricky time making it to the door. The pony skittered on the ice patches, despite her winter shoes. Normally, people had little bother navigating the roads around here. As County Councillor, he took pride in ensuring the clearing of roads—particularly ones that went through his land.

Bissett's mouth was a clenched line of anger by the time he made it to the rickety railing by the front door. The thawing parts of the yard bore the scars of his sleigh's runners.

"There you are!" Regina announced, her voice bright and brittle. "Come on up."

She tugged the old-fashioned wooden bucket to the steps. The horse sniffed at the frigid water with an affronted air.

Bissett ignored Regina and strode into the front hall. "Harriet? Harriet Roche! Where are you?"

"I'm here, George," she replied.

He frowned at the faintness in her voice. He peered into the kitchen where she sat in an old rocker by the heat of a gargantuan black stove.

"What's this about donating your land?" he asked. The kitchen was chill and damp, despite the size of the stove. The flue looked blocked.

She squinted at him. Her eyes had taken on a yellow glow since the last heart attack.

"Well, mother hasn't come to any firm decisions," Regina said, bustling past him and into the kitchen. "I mean to say—"

"I'm not sure it's any business of yours, George. Unless perhaps you want to buy it? Is that why you're here?"

He glared at her. "I've too much invested around here already to be buying up every scrap that comes up for sale."

"Is that right? I hear you're planning to buy three marsh lots and are part of the new drainage scheme. Isn't it illegal to buy more than one lot?"

He sat down at their plain kitchen table, making no reply.

Murmuring something about paying no attention to her mother, Regina took an enamel coffeepot from the stove and started filling him a cup. He looked into the black tar and took a tentative sip. Then he laughed.

"I've known you for how long, Harriet Roche? How many years? You never change. Michael would never have made a go of it without you. I've no desire on your farm, but I know the council will pay good money for it. Over fifteen thousand, I should say. You mightn't know it out here, there's an economic depression right now. You should take what money you can."

He finished his cup with a grimace.

Regina's eyes had gone round at the figure. "Mother. You should listen to Mr. Bissett."

"Bertie Wilson's chairman of the committee. He wants the contract to come out here for...Well, never mind. He owes me a favour and I'll make sure you get a good price. If you won't do it for your daughters, why not think of old Michael? The years you've put in here. To be handed over, just like that? Maybe you've gone soft in the head."

Harriet considered him, her upper lip protruding like a sulky child's. She and Michael had always hated Bissett. The way he lorded it over everyone. She knew there was some crafty scheme involved for his benefit.

"Well, I'm not so soft I cannot tell you to get out of—"

"Mother!" Regina said. "I won't have you speak to Mr. Bissett in that tone."

Harriet stared at her daughter. This impudence had started the other morning when Regina had refused to take her to live with Edgar.

"Mr. Bissett. My mother will need the proceeds from any sale to cover her...living expenses. Besides, there's the matter of the title. We're not sure the land is fully hers and we intend to contest it."

Bissett looked from mother to daughter. Both their faces reddened with anger, both prominent chins elevated with stubbornness. He considered the Roches an odd lot, but this was something else.

He stood up and left without saying another word.

Assessor

59 Maitland St, Halifax, March 19, 1886

"Emmett? Are you ever coming down?" his mother called from the bottom of the stairs.

He noted the impatience in her voice. With a heavy sigh, he put down the book he was trying to read. He lay in bed fully dressed, staring at the web of cracks on his sloped ceiling.

Principles of Psychology by Herbert Spencer tumbled to the floor. Emmett liked the idea of the book better than the reality of wading through the heavy prose. The stuffy old bookseller on Granville St. had looked down his spectacles when Emmett paid for it.

Out of boredom, he had filched a section of the flyleaf to roll tobacco. He hoped nobody would notice the smell if they came to rouse him. He considered rolling another before kicking off his eiderdown with frustration. He took a while to pick at a pimple, still suffering acne despite being twenty-five.

"Emmett?" came the call again. More insistent. If his mother wasn't coming herself, the next sally might be to send in the servant, Angela. Angela was over-familiar and often scolded the young scion.

He stomped to the door, opened it to roar down the stairs, "I'm coming!"

Why were they bothering him? It was a Saturday.

He looked out the hall window to the round corner of Saint George's, where his father preached. The church was renowned for being in the "Palladium Style". It reminded Emmett of an ornate lady's hatbox, the small nubbin of a spire like a squat handle perched on top. At the very top was a weather vane in the shape of Halley's comet. His father often used it as an image in his sermons. Emmett glowered at it before pounding downstairs.

There was a single bowl of porridge on the dining room table. It was as cold as the look Angela gave him as she bustled by.

"What time d'you call this?" she asked. "Your breakfast's already gone cold."

Angela's house-dress was shabby, and she only worked part-time. His father, as a vicar, could not afford a full-time servant.

"I'll have some of that coffee," Emmett said cheerily, giving her cheek a peck. "As dark as your beautiful cheek."

"Huh," she said, unimpressed. "It's your mother you should charm, son. Not me."

"Very right, Angela," his mother said, coming in from the kitchen with a coffeepot. "Now he's down, you'll see to his room?"

"Yes, ma'am." Angela headed upstairs, but was unable to resist calling back, "I'll be sure to open the window. Give it a good airing."

"You shouldn't encourage her, Emmett," his mother said, pouring the coffee. "She has far too many..."

"Liberties?" he supplied, sitting down.

"Notions. You should hear her on your prospects for marriage."

Emmett grimaced, sipping at his tepid coffee. "Ugh. I'd rather not know."

"We are all concerned about your..." His mother was always pausing, at a loss for words, waiting for someone else to supply them. Emmett remained stirring his cold porridge, not rising to the bait.

"Your lack of progress in that area," she continued. "Your father was just this morning wondering how—"

"Mother!" he erupted. "St-st-stop interfering in my private life? I'm a grown man now."

She paused, slowly putting linen into their scratched sideboard. She spoke calmly, as if to a young child having a tantrum. "Emmett. Calm yourself, please. Your father has said that as long as you live under our roof, you must obey our wishes. We wish you to marry and marry well."

His shoulders hunched like a cornered animal. "Well, what if no-one will have me?" he spat back. "Have you thought of that? None of the fine ladies of Halifax have any time for a penniless vicar's son."

"Watch your tone, young man! I'm sure we can find someone of our station who would be a fine match. Why, your father and I—"

"I don't want to hear it!"

"—Our marriage was arranged. Oh! You are intolerable. What about Rebecca Walker from your Dalhousie days?"

"She called me 'louche'. Or so I heard. And all her circle shunned me. Didn't like my sta-sta-stammer." He wasn't stammering now, just mocking himself. "She only spoke with me because she had to. She's in our congregation."

His mother made an exasperated sound as she sat down beside him. "Emmett. We just want you to be happy. You're too absorbed in books and...whatever it is you do all day in your room. Can't you see what a difference a nice girl would make to you? It has your poor father so vexed..."

Emmett snorted, face flushed. "V-v-vexed? My father wants me out, is why!"

She said nothing, her face an unmoving mask.

"He can't st-st-stand that I didn't finish that divinity degree. That I studied medicine instead."

"We agreed you would study for the church. Some money to pay for your tuition came from the congregation. Have you considered how disappointed they will be when they hear you're not following your father to the pulpit?"

"I don't care!"

"Emmett. Keep your voice down. Angela will hear."

"I don't care what Angela hears! Or what Becky Walker or anyone else in the st-st-stupid congregation thinks."

"You'll care if they come looking for repayment. Have you thought about taking a position to pay them back? You can't expect us to shield you forever."

He stood up.

"Look at you," his mother said, voice cold. "Behaving like a child and you a grown man of twenty-five. Where are you going?"

He wouldn't look back at her. "Wherever I please. I'm going out!"

He only had time to half-pull on his jacket before giving the hall door a dramatic slam behind him.

~

George Street, Halifax, March 28, 1886

"Hello? Anybody here?"

Emmett craned his neck, peering about the dusty government office. He looked again at the address on the note his father had thrust into his hand, eyes pure fury. Emmett at least had the satisfaction of seeing the mask of holy self-righteousness slip as his father issued his marching orders. He was to report to the Overseers office for work on Monday morning.

A thin shaft of sunlight broke through shuttered windows and stirred lazy dust motes. There were four wooden desks, in various states of disarray. Shelves of ledgers and dull-looking government books lined the walls. He had a sudden attack of dread and ducked back out the door, wishing to rush down the narrow stairs and back out onto Hollis Street.

Voices ascending the stairs blocked his escape.

"—Mr. Forbes is doing quite a business in the meat trade, from what I hear. Arthur, perhaps you might—"

The older man paused mid-sentence and looked up at Emmett from under bushy grey eyebrows. A lanky younger man with a prominent Adam's apple stood behind him.

"Maybe I'm in the wrong place," Emmett said. "I should leave."

"No, no," the older man insisted, scrutinizing him. "Do stay! We don't get many visitors here at the Office of the Overseers of the Poor."

"I'm supposed to report here. My father said—"

"Your *father*? And who might he be?"

He was level with Emmett now and thrust his gargantuan head near, sniffing loudly.

Emmett drew back, threatened even though the man hardly reached his shoulder. The large bulb of his red nose, pocked and purple-veined, was hideous enough to be frightening. The confined landing at the top of the stairs filled with an odour of whisky and damp.

"V-v-vicar Forrestall. From St. George's Church."

"Why, you're the man we're waiting all morning for! You must be young Emmett. Arthur here came in extra early to prepare the office for your arrival. Didn't you, Arthur?"

Emmett wondered at the state of the office before Arthur's cleaning.

"Please, enter before me. The working day may begin, now you are here."

Bewildered, Emmett backed into the room.

"And," he managed. "Who might you be?"

"Robert Mitchener is my name. I *might* be Treasurer of the Overseers."

Emmett swallowed and nodded, fumbling with his leather satchel. He used to carry it to classes at Dalhousie. Now it was conspicuously empty.

Mitchener lowered his rotund form into a nearby chair as young Arthur sidled by. Letting the silence stretch out, Mitchener stared at Emmett for a time. With great deliberation, he patted his tweed waistcoat, retrieving from various pockets pipe, penknife and pouch. Laying them before him on the desk, he only looked away to scrape at the dottle in the bowl of his pipe, making a great show of scrutinizing the operation.

Emmett noted a fine snow of dandruff beneath the old man's unkempt curly salt-and-pepper hair.

Satisfied, Mitchener spat into the pipe and loudly sucked it back out, expectorating the juice into a can beside his desk.

"Forrestall?" he mused. "Think I know him to see. I go to St. Paul's myself."

He motioned with his pipe in the general direction of the nearby church.

"Yes. St. Paul's. I used to drop in there when at college. It's just across the square. Or it was. I mean. They've moved it, haven't they?"

"Moved St. Paul's!" Mitchener exclaimed. "Things have changed a lot in Halifax since we joined Canada, but they haven't taken to transporting places of worship."

"Of course, I mean the College. Across from the church. They've moved it. It's no longer...Oh."

He realized by the glimmer in Mitchener's eye that he was being mocked. He thought he heard a stifled snicker from Arthur, his nose buried in a box of documents.

"Look," Emmett said, "I should go."

"No, no, no. Sit down there, lad. We're just having a bit of sport. This tends to be a dull office. Mostly Arthur and myself having a tedious time of it. Most of the other Overseers are from other departments of the civil service. They only drop by when they need to look up a deed or something. Sit!"

Mitchener uttered his command with a tinge of menace. Emmett sank into a rickety chair.

"What shall I do here?" he asked, voice meek.

"Oh, what to do?" Mitchener sighed. He was once again busy with his pipe, tamping down his foul-smelling tobacco. He fetched around for a means to ignite the stuff.

Emmett couldn't resist producing his box of lucifers and offering it. His superior considered the box before smiling, lighting the bowl and inhaling slowly to redden its contents. He exhaled with satisfaction.

"That's a good start," he said. "We'll find ways of making you useful. Put that expensive Dalhousie education to work."

He pocketed the matchbox with a smile.

"I st-st-studied as much arts and science as I could," Emmett blurted. "Not just theology. The new science of psychology was a particular interest."

Mitchener tapped his teeth with the pipe stem, uninterested. "Any good with the martial arts? They teach you how to knock a few heads?"

Emmett looked shocked while Arthur laughed.

"*You've* developed a bit of a knack for that, haven't you Arthur my lad?"

"Oh no, sir," said the diffident young man. "Well, maybe that one time."

"But," Emmett intruded, exasperated. "You're Overseers of the Poor. What do you mean by knocking heads?"

"Oh, the poor are all right. It's the ones who have to pay for them you'll be knocking heads with. They'll want to knock yours in when they see how you assess their land for taxes. We've had to increase the poor tax ever since that monstrosity of a poorhouse burnt down on South Street. Not popular around this town. Not to worry. We'll have you doing assessments of people in no time."

He peered again at Emmett through the thickening fog of pipe smoke, deciding. "Don't think we should have you doing Collection, anyway. We also have the authority to enforce upkeep of any indigent, by family members with means. What else? Oh, and we may legally bind anyone to give up their children into apprenticeship or servitude until they reach the age of majority. We must ensure someone educates them. Legally."

"Truly?" Emmett said, surprised at such power. "Who would submit to such slavery? Even America has outlawed such unchristian practices."

Mitchener kept the pipe in his mouth despite gaping at Emmett. Arthur walked over, stiffly placing a ledger on the desk.

Emmett realized he had made another gaffe. He felt a sudden cold sweat of shame.

"Here are the details on Forbes, sir," Arthur murmured. Ignoring Emmett, he exited to a back room.

Mitchener sighed and also stood. "Arthur has been my ward for several years," he said in a quiet tone. "He is a fine apprentice and you would do well to remember it, *if* you are to remain in this office. Now, let's find you a desk."

Aboiteau

Squire Bissett Farmhouse, Cole Harbour, April, 1886

"Honestly, can't see how to square it, Bissett." John Watson shook his head, draining the last of George Bissett's rum from a glass. "'fraid I must go back to the shareholders in Sunderland with this news."

Bissett studied the Englishman's corpulent features. George couldn't decide which he despised most, the man's high accent, his constant drinking, or his inadequacy as a business partner. He kept his face impassive.

"We can fix that aboiteau. They just need to extend us a bit more money."

Watson shook his head, slowly coming to a conclusion as he studied his empty glass by the kitchen lantern's light.

"Maybe. Yes. You're right. I'll take a trip back and see," he said, belching softly. He arose from the kitchen table. "Awfully good of you to put me up each time I'm over. Well, better head for bed."

"Don't mention it. Anything to save the company's money."

There was a grim set to Bissett's thin lips as he watched the Englishman fumble upstairs. He reminded George of a heavy schoolboy nicknamed Fatty from George's distant childhood. They had bullied him mercilessly. Bissett had stayed out of it, although he enjoyed observing how the class needed to have someone suffer. His wife, Sophia, had given Watson their bedroom, so they were sleeping in a smaller room: the room his mother died in last year.

He reached up to quench the lantern and fumbled his own way upstairs.

The bedroom door creaked as he tried slipping in quietly. Sophia had the curtains pulled tight, making the room black as a coffin. He crept toward the beds, stubbing his stockinged toe on the little side table. He stifled a curse.

"George," she snapped.

"You're awake," he said, sitting down on his little bed with a grunt. They had moved the children's old beds in here. She kept a gap between hers and his.

"Is he gone to bed?" she whispered.

He sighed, removing his breeches. "Yes. No more rum left."

"What was he saying?"

"Wants to go back to England and talk to the shareholders."

"That's bad, George."

In the darkness, George looked over at her. He saw nothing but imagined her features. They were still handsome despite her advancing years: her silvering hair didn't show as much through the straw blonde; her pale face had a *craquelure* of wrinkles, like expensive porcelain. He considered her his finest possession.

"George?" she pressed. "What are we to do? James says you'll lose everything."

"James knows nothing of business."

"It doesn't take a genius to see the dyked land is failing. Flooded again."

"What exactly did your brother say? *He's* the one I asked to oversee the dykes."

"Keep it down," she hissed. "Our guest will hear you!"

"Our guest is snoring off my rum," George said, lowering his voice all the same. "Which I had to ply him with to calm him down about your useless brother's mistakes."

She rebuked him with silence. Or so George interpreted it. Her soft hiccup of a sob surprised him.

"Don't punish James. He...he means well. Dad was so hard on him."

He sighed and reached out, clumsily patting her shoulder.

"Sophia, your brother is the least of our worries. If the company defaults on us, I must let him go."

He felt her stiffen.

"You are not to punish him!" her voice was hard, with an edge of hysteria. "I want you to promise it."

"Don't worry," he soothed, "I'll find him something else. You and I might end in the poorhouse, but your pet brother will still..."

It was George's turn to fall silent. A thought struck him. Sophia turned on her side, facing him.

"What is it?" she asked, fear in her voice. "You're not thinking of sending Eunice and James to the poorhouse?"

"Shush," he said with a chuckle. He was a great admirer of his own humour and planning. "'Am I my brother's keeper?' Or brother-in-law's keeper?"

"Whatever are you saying?"

"The Poor Farm. It'll need a Keeper. Better have him destroying the County's property than mine."

The Dean

Dalhousie College Building, Carleton Street, Halifax, 2nd June, 1886

Sweating, Emmett struggled to pedal the black bicycle up the steep end of Sackville Street. Once it levelled off past the Citadel, he hoped not to have such a hard time. Slowing with the exertion, he wondered if they would allow him to take a shortcut through the Public Gardens.

This new Rover bicycle was all black, spindly and shining like a giant insect. The council had purchased several for official business. He had pleaded with Mitchener to let him take one out. The latter only grunted assent when Emmett insisted he knew how to operate one and that it would spare having to expense a street tram.

BOOM!

The explosion echoed down from the grass-covered hill to his right. He wobbled on the bike and fell into the gutter. For a flash, he was sure someone had shot him.

Then he saw street urchins on Dresden Row laughing at him. The noon gun. The old thing was a cannon on *H.M.S. Shannon* when it captured the *Chesapeake* in the War of 1812.

This stupid town, he cursed to himself as he dusted down his clothes, so stuck in its military past. His trousers bore smears of oil from the new bicycle chain. His satchel was even dirtier, having taken the brunt of his fall.

After he walked most of the rest of the way, the new college loomed before him. It rose above a broad stretch of fields scarred by cart ruts and other tracks; the ground sodden from the recent spring rain.

Emmett had not bothered to come see the college when it was under construction. The modern edifice impressed him: four stories of blood-red brick with long grey windows and a tall central tower. There were no students in view.

He picked his way through the muck, past fresh saplings surrounded by iron railings. He parked the Rover against a nearby tree. A perfect half-circle stone arch and fanlight crowned the main door at the base of the college's tower. As he approached, he felt the tower peering down at him in disapproval.

Inside, the new lobby was cool and hushed. At the far end, a broad oak staircase split to the left and right, rising to the floor above. The banisters shone with new varnish. Emmett whistled to himself. What a difference from the cramped squalor of his college days.

The quietness of the place unnerved him. Where should he go? He wandered up the double stairs for two floors until he spotted a door with a small square of paper pinned to it: "Dean's Office" written in an ornate hand. He tapped on the half-open door.

"Hello?" he asked, peering in.

"Yes?"

Emmett went cold with recognition, his face drained several shades paler. *What was she doing here?* And in this well-appointed new office?

"*Becky*? I mean, Rebecca? Do you remember me? We met a few times at the Dalhousie socials."

"Emmett?" She affected recognition. "How are you?"

"Ah, fine. I didn't expect you here. I mean, they don't allow girls at the college now, do they?"

Her brow furrowed as she gazed at him coldly. "I work here. I am Dr. Reid's secretary. Can I help you with anything?"

He was suddenly conscious of his shabby appearance, covered in mud and oil and sweating from traipsing here from town. He put a guilty hand through his greasy black hair. He still fantasized about her regularly and by the cold, hard stare she fixed on him, he feared she might be reading his thoughts.

"Right...Of course. Actually, I'm here to see the Dean. Dr. Reid. I mean..."

"You are?" she asked, unconvinced.

He remembered now being drunk at one of those socials, blurting out a request to dance. The titters of her friends and the look she gave as she replied with a chilling "Certainly".

"I, ah...I work for the council now. Overseers of the Poor. The Doctor wanted to consult about—"

"I see," she said, standing up. He recalled the elegant way she stood to take his clammy hand, at the dance.

"Would you?" he blurted. "Would you like to meet later? To catch up. Perhaps lunch? It's a v-v-very..."

Oh, did he have to say *very*?

She looked him over with icy disdain, before opening the door behind her. The contempt in her gaze was plain to read. "Dr. Reid is this way."

A profound odour hit Emmett—a tang of orange and tobacco—as he meekly followed her into the large office. Past a rich mahogany desk, a large window commanded a vista of the city down to the harbour and beyond. Alongside half-filled bookshelves was a workbench covered with tools and disassembled devices: clocks, microscopes, even a camera. Emmett noticed, amidst the jumble, a bald porcelain bust covered with swatches of paper with scribbled Latin terms.

A burly man with a graying beard bent intently over the Phrenology head, consulting his notebook. He wore a dressing gown and slippers.

"Yes?" he said, looking at them over his spectacles.

"Dr. Reid," Rebecca said, "this gentleman is from the Overseers of the Poor."

Reid looked puzzled, moving his mouth back and forth as he chewed on something.

"The Poor Farm," Emmett ventured. "I was sent by Mr. Mitchener. The Treasurer. To consult on the design?"

Reid flashed him a sudden smile, teeth stained an alarming yellow. Emmett realized he must chew tobacco. He noticed a half-peeled orange on the workbench. Alongside it was an ashtray full of raw tobacco, some peel stirred in.

"And who might you be?" Reid said.

"Emmett Forestall," Rebecca supplied. She tilted her head in his direction before leaving the room.

"Yes," Emmett said hurriedly. "I have the proposals for the new Poor Farm."

By way of explanation, he indicated his beaten leather satchel.

"Come, sit down," Reid said with a chuckle, pointing to a chair by his desk. "What do you think of our Rebecca? Quite the ice princess, eh?"

Emmett sat down, staring nervously out at the view. "Actually. I know Miss Walker from my college days."

He blinked as Reid sat down in front of him, briefly blocking the sunlight. "Oh? Do tell, young man."

Reid's mouth was full of tobacco, and his voice sounded slushy to Emmett. He didn't know where to look. "She's not really a friend," was all he could say.

"Too bad," Reid said. He ruminated for a while. "You studied at the old college? What did you take?"

"Theology, mostly. But I tried to take in other subjects. I attended some of your lectures on St-st-stirpiculture."

It surprised Emmett to notice the stammer didn't register on Reid's face.

"A cleric dipping into my classes," Reid exclaimed. "That is unusual! What did you think?"

"I don't know. There was a lot to take in."

"The key idea. What did you think of the key idea?"

Emmett gave him a blank look.

"The *fundamental* idea," Reid said. "Superior and inferior strains make up our Society. The inferior are unfit and we should protect and contain them. They cannot take part in life, so we must do what we can for the lesser amongst us. This may even include sterilization."

"How do you know?" Emmett said. The Dean's zealous tone reminded him of his father's sermons. "How do you know who is lesser?"

Reid scoffed.

"If you could see some of the specimens I have in Mount Hope, you would know."

He waved across the harbour to where the large asylum brooded on a brow of a hill in the distance, then returned his gaze to Emmett.

"Imagine we were to breed you with Miss Walker," he said. "What traits would your offspring inherit?"

Emmett stared at the distant asylum in Dartmouth, too embarrassed to look Reid in the eye.

"Why, good ones," the Doctor continued with a chuckle. "You are both fit young people. Now imagine we were to breed either of you with some of my feeble-minded inmates? Or, worse yet, with one of the lesser races that clog up our institutions."

Reid shook his head. A thin tobacco-yellowed bubble of spittle settled on his lip.

Emmett considered for a moment and swallowed. "What about helping them?" he asked, meekly. He knew he should let the man finish his bluster but some part of himself couldn't help it.

Reid narrowed his eyes. "You haven't been at this long, have you? Nine years I've been Superintendent at Mount Hope. Such dregs of humanity I've seen. You'll understand when you've been at this for longer."

Reid frowned, noticing the spittle on his beard and wiping it off. "I used to think it was the environment, their impoverished circumstances, that was to blame. But believe me, that is not the key factor. As Darwin has shown us, the parents determine the beast: lion, lamb or snake."

Emmett was looking down now. Ashamed but not knowing why.

Reid paused, considering. "Cheer up, young man," he said. "You are no longer one of my undergraduates. Besides, the reason you are here is for the inoffensive ones. Not the ones dangerous to themselves or others. We have Mount Hope for that. No, a poor farm is the thing for the harmless insane. I'm excited the government is behind this. It took no small amount of lobbying on our behalf. Now, why don't you show me that proposal."

Without a word, Emmett rummaged about in his satchel to retrieve a dossier with the stamp of the Council on it and handed it over.

Reid peered at the document, muttering as he read aloud. He seemed to forget Emmett was present. "Good location, about 6 miles east of the asylum...300 acres... Not sure what kind of condition existing buildings are in...This location is wrong...Should be upon and not under the rising ground...Wooden frame main building, with dug basement containing the kitchen? No. No. No. Kitchen should be a separate building. Fire hazard. Some of them might cook but...Sixteen small dormitory rooms... Many for Violents... No! This is all wrong."

He looked up, staring hard at Emmett.

"Aren't you taking this down, man?"

"I? I'm sorry. Didn't realize."

He fished in his pocket for a small copybook and a stub of a pencil.

"There is no need to separate them so much," Reid continued. "Or to be so concerned for the violent. Those will be in Mount Hope. No. This is all wrong. Change it to open dormitories, for ventilation. Didn't the council learn anything from the fire at the last poor house?"

Emmett kept nodding and scribbling random words, afraid to speak.

"Sexes strictly segregated, naturally. As discussed: we don't want them breeding! There may be a single strong room for the occasional Violent. Perhaps another couple of rooms for the unclean or undesirable. Yes, no access to either sex. Except through the Superintendent's quarters. Best even to have separate kitchens. Keep buildings separate but with...hmm...covered passageways connecting... Are you getting all this?"

Bewildered, Emmett kept nodding. He had written nothing for a while. His mind had drifted to Rebecca. He sat up with a start.

"Oh! Uhm...'Room for Occasional V-V-Violents'... Ahm..."

Reid made an angry squirting noise, spitting tobacco into a jar he kept on his desk. "Miss Walker," he called out.

"Can you come in for some dictation?" He looked at Emmett with disappointment. "Perhaps you should go. I will send my response to Council separately. Has it gone to tender?"

"Yes," Emmett replied with a guilty nod.

Reid made an exasperated sound. "Then why send you? Ugh, you are the very embodiment of their incompetence. I thought you a better representative of this College."

Rebecca opened the door. Both men looked at her with expectation. She arched an eyebrow.

"Very well," Reid said with a sigh. "Tell Mitchener to delay any tenders. I will get a response to you soon."

Emmett looked from Rebecca back to Reid.

"You may go," Reid said.

Emmett stood, pocketing his notebook. He couldn't help but notice the look of pleasure on Rebecca's face as he rushed out.

Keeper

*Poor Farm (formerly Harriet Roche's), Cole Harbour,
August 26, 1886*

James Turner cast down his scythe. The blade was dull,
and he had no whetstone. Sunlight gleamed on the snath,
the worn wooden shaft. He was wearing an old straw hat
to keep the sun from burning his bald pate. He took it off
and wiped away the sweat with the back of his hand. He
flopped down onto the stubble he had cleared and
cupped his hands about his mouth.

"Enough," he yelled to his sons. "Tell your mother to
bring up a bite."

The two boys stopped stooking sheaves downhill from
him and sauntered off towards the old Roche farmhouse.
His eyes wandered over the bowed roof. He didn't need
years of carpentering to see that the whole thing would
have to come down.

With a sigh, he stretched himself, looking up to the
blue bowl of sky overhead. Stifling heat radiated down,
with no cooling breeze from the estuary. Not a bird or
cloud stirred through the azure haze.

"It's boiling for rain," James mumbled to himself, de-
feated by the humidity. He took a deep breath and closed
his eyes. He could take a quick nap, he thought, a few
minutes' respite from gathering half-spoiled hay and
worrying about fixing buildings and fences. He felt
around for his hat to drowse under. Where was it? Opening one eye, he squinted to his left.

The colt cantered up the hill and past his vision. He was up in a moment, hallooing for the others to come back and help. Of all the animals gone wild about the old farm, he dearly wanted to capture this one. He was a bay with the look of having been a fine beast.

Although James had lost his own farm ten years before, he never lost a farmer's revulsion at having animals loose. What if black bear or grey wolf got at him? The bay's flanks had a sheen in the high sunlight. He could make out the horse's ribs. It must be feeble from lack of proper feeding.

Thirty feet from the animal, he stopped his jog and spread his arms. "Shush now," he said in a calming voice, despite his fast breathing. "It's alright, big fellow."

The colt looked at him with large mistrustful eyes, nose pointed uphill, ready to bolt.

"Alright now," James soothed, pulling a hank of grass and holding it out.

The colt's black tail flicked. He turned his head to look at James.

"James!" Eunice shouted from below him. "Here's your lunch."

James made a futile dive in the horse's direction as it bolted. He saw the animal's eyes register fear as it gave him one last look before disappearing into the trees. They would never catch it in there.

"That colt," he said, through gritted teeth. "The one I've been trying to catch."

"Well," said Eunice. "Shouting and cursing after it won't help!"

He collapsed back down in the grass. Eunice put a basket down between them and arranged her skirts before sitting. There was a bottle of milk capped with newspaper, a hank of bread and some early russet apples from the little orchard by the shore. His stomach rumbled.

"Where's your hat, James?" Eunice asked. "If you're not careful, the top of your head will burn up. A man your age has to mind himself. Leave the running around after live-stock to your sons."

He had recently turned sixty. It was cause for reflection: along with the hair gone from the top of his head, there were many chances he wished he could have back. As was his way, he said nothing.

"Besides," she continued. "Today's a Sunday. Do you want the minister complaining about us again? 'Keep holy the Sabbath.' Did you hear what Sophia heard him say? Right outside the church door? 'A lot of strange doings up at the old Roche farm, at all hours of the day and night.'"

His eyes were closed, in an attempt to ignore her. He also heard the concern in her voice under the harangue. Wearily, he made to placate her. "Eunice, we should be more worried about my brother-in-law than that fool of a minister."

There. He said it. Hadn't the founder of the Methodist church stressed criticism of doctrine?

"What do you mean? It's thanks to George we have this work. Would you prefer to be out on the road looking for a job again? People know about your involvement with that failing dam. And they're saying you're doing nothing up here. Just lying around idle, letting the hay spoil and the animals run wild."

He pondered for a long while, eyes closed. Losing his family farm was a hollow pain that never left. It wasn't his fault. Everyone had struggled back then. Farms in Upper Canada or Argentina did things cheaper and were more abundant than here. Hard winters and flinty soil meant Nova Scotian farmers couldn't compete with cheap produce coming in by train. The world shrank, and they were the victims of it.

George had smirked at him the first time they walked the Poor Farm together. The state of the fences. The wildness of the animals. It slowly sunk in how difficult the task was. When he asked for more help, George airily said he would see what Council could do. Nothing came of it. Eunice had forgotten all the toil of the last couple of months because a few tongues were wagging.

James should get indignant about the unfairness of it all, but preferred not to speak unless he had to. He had mostly been a bystander in the dam scheme, while George Bissett was knee deep in blame. Somehow, his sister and Eunice had contrived to make the whole failed project his fault. No doubt it would be the same this time around.

"It's not the Roche farm," he said.

"What?" snapped Eunice. She hated his interminable silences, but hated his odd declarations more.

"It's the Poor Farm," he said, sitting up to look into her basket.

She watched bemused as he rooted about, pulling out the biggest of the stunted apples. She noticed his beard had a fleck of straw in it, right at the greyest part. Without a word, she reached over and removed it. He half-smiled at her and bit off a part of the apple, masticating loudly.

Council

Halifax County Courthouse, Spring Garden Road, Halifax, January 17th, 1887

George Bissett, eyes drooping with utter boredom, stared out the courtroom window at falling snow. Flakes swirled about on the stiff breeze, a welcome contrast to the dead atmosphere inside. The warden tended to a black stove that hissed in one corner. An old wreck of a man, he would trudge out of the room without notice, returning with a small bucket of glistening black coal. *Why couldn't he just get a bigger bucket?* George wondered.

W. H. Wiswell, Clerk of the Municipality, seated beside the Chair, was in the middle of reading a report into the record. It was a long tedious recommendation for someone as License Inspector for Elmsdale. Wiswell's voice was as monotonous as a papist reading out the mass in Latin.

George rolled his eyes and surveyed his fellow councillors, squeezed onto the benches for lawyers and criminals. He snorted to himself. An appropriate spot for them. The council was meeting here until they finished the new building on Grand Parade.

"The Council will now open the floor to general questions," the Clerk announced in his faltering voice. A large portrait of the Queen hung above him. Her glum face looked to the left, ignoring them. She was even unmoved at the start of proceedings when they had all pledged God to save her.

Councillor Cruikshank stood. Bissett pursed his lips in tight displeasure. The fellow could have dressed better for a council meeting. He looked like he had just been stoking hay for cattle.

"I would like to raise the issue of a misuse of Council funds," he announced.

This awoke several Councillors from their slumbers. George straightened up.

"That is a serious allegation," the Chair replied, frowning down at Cruikshank from his raised Judge's seat. "Can the member from Little River provide more detail?"

"Yes," Cruikshank said, scratching the back of his head. He faltered, an amateur actor forgetting his lines. "The Poor Farm in Cole Harbour. Where has all that money gone?"

George raised his hand. At a nod from the Chair, he cleared his throat.

"The funds were approved last April and have been well managed by the Committee on Public Property. As the honourable member from Little River is well aware. A full report is forthcoming—"

Councillor Sellars jumped to his feet. Bissett narrowed his eyes. Here was the source of the attack.

"I disagree," Sellars said, at a volume not far from a shout. "My district cannot sit by while Council wastes so much money on this... this," in his fluster, he sought for the word, "boondoggle out in Cole Harbour."

"The honourable member from West Chezzetcook has the floor," the Chair announced.

Sellars straightened himself, took a deep breath. He had dressed properly, George noted.

"There is a Keeper being paid $16 a month while no work has yet begun on that farm. A farm purchased—"

A few "Hear hears!" supported Sellars' pause.

"Purchased," he continued, cheeks aflame. "Under questionable circumstances. It's January now, and the Committee is doing who knows what in sorting out the construction tender. I propose the Council abandon this elaborate fraud and look for a better use of public money."

Sellars, thought George, grinding his teeth. That fat innkeeper had always objected to the farm. He had got a few more to support his gripe.

George looked meaningfully at Bertie Wilson, their committee chairman. Wilson's replying smile was bland and serene.

"A motion has been called for," Wiswell called out, struggling to make his faint voice heard. "Mr. Sellars, will you repeat the motion to enter it into the record?"

Sellars patted his protruding belly, producing a handwritten note from his waistcoat.

"Yes, yes. That 'we object to the excessive expenditure at the Cole Harbour location. We motion that the property be sold and proceeds paid back to the County Treasurer.'"

He concluded his reading with satisfaction, a smug schoolboy.

"Objection," Wilson called out in his leisurely drawl. "Point of Order."

Wiswell frowned in his direction, and Bertrand Wilson drew himself upright. He was lanky, with straw-coloured hair, and carried himself foppishly.

"The honourable members from Little River and West Chezzetcook cannot reverse a committee decision without first having the Committee's full report available."

Most of the chamber made some commotion to this. It was hard to tell if cat-calls out-weighed the hear-hears. Wilson waited for silence.

"We have some minor alterations to make in finishing the report. Which we hope—" Wilson paused disdainfully as Sellars brayed his objections. "Which we hope to present for Wednesday's sitting. May I say that the work to procure a farm for the benefit of the harmlessly insane and blamelessly indigent has been conducted with great diligence. Including consultation with Dr. Reid of Dalhousie. How quickly the honourable member from West Chezzetcook forgets the findings of Commissioner Bell, presented last year to our provincial assembly. Auctioning of the poor for work to the lowest bidder! Disgraceful practices that cannot continue. Our poor farm will be of significant benefit to the public purse and to those members of society who need the most help. A fact that other members ignore—" chorus of objections and support. "And have no viable alternative to."

Wilson sat back down, folding his arms with a satisfied air.

"Very well, Mr. Wilson," the Clerk said. "We will postpone the motion until the report is published and circulated to all members."

"What about the outstanding legal issues? Around the land?" Sellars sputtered. George wondered if the man might have a seizure. His fleshy features were apoplectic.

"The Clerk of the court will undertake to investigate all legal matters," Wiswell said with a sigh.

"Can someone at least explain to the Council why there needs to be a man employed at over..." Sellars made an exasperated search through his papers, the puce tinge to his cheeks abating. "...Over sixteen dollars per month to do nothing, out there by the sea?"

George wondered if he should say something. It was a delicate matter with James Turner being his brother-in-law. Wilson was smirking at him, an eyebrow arched. *He knew.*

"Has no member of the Committee a valid answer to the member's concern?" the Clerk asked, voice mournful.

Edmond Ryan, Councillor from Lower Prospect and fellow Committee member, came to George's rescue. "If I may," he ventured. "I have heard there is still much work out there. The man is not idle, as there is a need for a person to oversee the place. Keeping hay in the barn and so on. The insurance policy insists on a Keeper to maintain the property."

Ryan's words are drowned out by a chorus of "Objection" and "For Shame". The Committee looked at one another with silent surprise. Their report had better be a good one.

~

The bailiff rubbed his hands, blowing into them for warmth. George brushed past the uniformed man as he exited the courthouse gloom. A phalanx of snarling stone lions and bearded gods gazed down on them, their features obscured by snow.

Bertie Wilson squinted up at the sandstone facade. "What do you suppose they represent, George?"

George, mind occupied, only grunted. He didn't care much about the abstract symbols of justice. He scowled at the pile of St. Mary's Cathedral down the hill. *Upstart Papists,* he groused to himself.

It was his habit to think this whenever he noted the gleaming white building. He reflected on how times had changed. Why couldn't they deport all these misfits as they did with the French over a hundred years ago? No need for any poor house to squeeze some work out of them: just expel them.

Across from the courthouse was a field of waste ground. The old poor house had stood there years before. He hoped the city leaving it idle was intended as a rebuke to the parish. A few horses from the nearby barracks tramped around the wet snow there. The ground was one big pauper graveyard, as far as he knew.

George felt one of his feet slip on the slick courthouse step.

"Careful there, George," Bertie said.

This did nothing to soften George's foul mood. He straightened himself and scanned the street, covered with several inches of fresh snow. It blurred the horse and carriage tracks. Also hiding any horseshit from view, George thought. He hated spring and the attendant melting of snow. It made Halifax smell like an ill-kept barn.

"We've a lot to talk about," George said tersely. "Out of earshot." He jerked his head, indicating the severe courthouse behind them.

"Agreed," Bertie said. "Best go down by the wharves. I know a spot. It's crawling with bloody Irish and sailors. Or worse," he chuckled. "Irish sailors. Anyway, too many of our crowd about the usual spots on Barrington."

George said nothing, gingerly stepping out onto the street. The road sweepers had shovelled the recent heavy snow along this side. It wouldn't do to get stuck in there.

They walked down the hill in silence, the cemetery everyone called the Old Burying Ground to their right. The black headstones and bare trees stood out from the quiet snow. A lion stood atop an arch commemorating the Crimean war.

Bertie noticed George looking across at it. "You'd think lions were native to Halifax," he joked. "There are so many statues about."

George made no reply, crossing Barrington to the pilastered front of the Academy of Music. Barrington Street was busy, although it looked like the weather had halted the trams. People huddled by, dodging wet snow falling off awnings. The odd horse and cart waited by a shop, delivering goods. Their owners often covered the beasts with a damp blanket; steam from their backs mingling with the cloud of their breath.

Turning down Salter Street, George noted the tall telegraph poles strung with wires descending to the harbour. They reminded him of the spars of the distant ships floating below. Halifax so loved ships that it brought them up the hill and into its streets.

"There's always Albemarle Street," Bertie mused.

George sighed. "One of the upper streets the reformers are trying to shut down? The one with all the taverns and brothels?"

"Yes."

"Too many soldiers. And too far in this weather."

"True."

George said no more, hurrying down the hill. The buildings turned more utilitarian the closer they got to Wood's Wharf: warehouses, dry goods stores and ship outfitters.

At the corner of Lower Water, the fug from the brewery assailed his nostrils. There had been complaints to the council about "unpleasant odours". Somebody looking for a donation from the Keith family, he supposed.

Bertie stopped at a nondescript building with darkened windows. The sign reading *The Sailor's Rest* direly needed repainting. "Here we are," he said.

An elderly black man stood shivering by the entrance. His clothes were filthy and ill-suited to the cold. He looked as if he were about to ask for something, then thought better of it.

The door opened to a small vestibule with a handwritten sign advertising room rates. There was no-one at the small desk.

They walked through to the saloon and stood by the large hearth to warm up. There was sawdust all over the stone floor. Mismatched shabby tables and chairs arrayed before a long counter.

The proprietor, a thin nervous man, appeared from the gloom. "Make yourselves at home, gentlemen," he called. "I'll be over in a moment."

"Can't understand why he's busy," George grumbled. "There's nobody here."

"At least it's quiet," Bertie said. "And the grog's good. He has some connection to Keith's and gets it fresh."

George picked the table nearest the blazing fire and sat down. Bertie Wilson sat across from him after a minute of shaking off damp snow and further warming up. George noticed the man's fair hair was thinning, worse even than his own.

"I know old Doull. Runs this hostelry," Bertie said with a weary sigh. "He doesn't get that many sailors in his rooms. The money's all in the tavern. I encourage him to take in some poorer souls to help ease the plight of the homeless."

"Commendable," George said dryly.

"Now gentleman, what will you have?" the barkeep said. He sounded breathless.

"Two pints of your finest," Bertie said. "Oh, before you rush off. We noticed an old darkie hanging around outside. Best move him on. Not good for business, I'm sure."

"Certainly, sir."

George licked his lips at the thought of the beer. He didn't indulge much, hating the fact that he liked it. A vision came into his mind of the bitter golden liquid—the miracle of how the acrid hoppy flavour would transform to warmth in his belly in a little while.

"*That* turned out to be an interesting morning."

Bertie's words interrupted his musings. George narrowed his eyes. "Listen, Wilson. That farm was your idea to begin with: keep it all legitimate and holy, consult that fool Reid at the college. Now we've got Sellars braying to pull the funding and your brother still fooling about with the construction."

"Now, now," Bertie said, holding his hands up. "Turns out things have improved for our John. He has too much to do with the sawmill construction. My brother will build it for you, but it won't be the grand plans the Dean was proposing."

"John Wilson is a disgrace," George hissed. He stopped, noting a young boy coming with their beer.

He sat back while the child served them in silence, visibly grinding his teeth, then continued when the boy was out of earshot. "A disgrace! He got greedy and bid too high for the tender. What he has built is either half-done or wrong. Even my fool of a brother-in-law can see that. James told me—"

"Ah, James," Bertie said. He took an infuriating sip of beer. "You're going to have a problem there."

"What do you mean?"

"Simple conflict of interest. You heard Sellars at the end."

"So what? James is doing a fine job."

"And his association with your failed dam. Could embarrass—"

"What are you saying?" George kept his voice quiet. He looked down, saw the drink and gulped back a portion—the expected bitterness welcome.

"I'm saying help me out." Bertie leaned back, looking around the vacant room. "Ryan's all right, but the others on the committee might get nervous. My brother needs help just as your James does—"

"Your brother in the family construction company," George scoffed.

"Yes. But I need you to help with calming the rest of the committee. We can probably pull through this if they line up behind a favourable report. And," Bertie paused for emphasis, "I will get Sellars to back off on the matter of your brother-in-law as keeper."

"How will you do that?"

Bertie tapped his nose. "Never you mind. Might have to involve lawyers. Wiswell, that wet lamb of a clerk, is getting interested in the land titles. Thought you had sorted the widow out?"

George took another swig, massaging his upper lip with his lower. "I thought I had, too." He shook his head. "The Roches are an odd family."

"Anyway, the chief thing is to stick together and not lose our calm." Bertie was smiling broadly, happy to have George Bissett back on board. "You go talk to Burgess and Chipman. See what Sellars has been saying to them. Just make sure there is no more talk of rescinding the construction tender."

He paused, looking at George in expectation.

George took another slug of beer. *There*, he thought, savouring the amber liquid: *the bitterness had faded*.

On Wednesday, a narrow majority received and adapted their report. Fourteen 'For' and twelve 'Against'.

Enclosure

Poor Farm, Cole Harbour, April 1889

It was after supper. The food had been bland and cold: suet and watery potatoes. They all sat at the long wooden tables of the dining room, some talking low.

"What do you have there?" Sally asked, walking over to the mute boy. The inmates had finished tidying up and Sally was checking nobody had kept anything sharp to hurt themselves with. Matron was quite careful about that sort of thing.

It was a small bit of ceramic, the stem of a clay pipe, white and blue. Sally had spotted him playing with it earlier, when the inmates were out exercising in the enclosure. He held it cupped in his hand.

"Where'd he get that?" Jenny, one of the longest-serving inmates, asked from the women's table. Her voice had the usual nasty edge to it, fear someone else was getting something she wasn't.

Sally leaned closer to peer at what he held. She was concerned the shard might be sharp.

His hands were a blur as he lashed out. Sally saw fear in his eyes.

She sprang back, hand to her face. There was blood trickling from her nose.

"Did he *hit* you?" Jenny's voice was hysterical, a mix of fear and laughter.

"It's all right. It's all right," Sally said, her voice muffled as she held her apron to her nose.

"Go get Andrew," Jenny yelled. "He can't be here. He can't be hitting out at us. He's too crazy."

Sally noted the reactions of the room with concern. The Normals: the ones who were just poor and not Insane, quick and quiet, stepped back from the ruckus. Some were from the same family and ended up here for the same reason: a drunk father in the Rockwell or a mother separated by the court. A lot of the Insane were oblivious, stuck in the same futile ritual, food dribbling down their chins.

Andrew MacDonald rushed in, looking about wildly. "What's all the noise? Is anyone hurt?"

Although untrained for the work, Andrew tried to be kind, cajoling the inmates where possible. Unlike Hugh Morash, a farm labourer who sometimes helped with inmates. Sally once saw Hugh belting inmates on the sly as if they were cattle.

"What happened to Sally?" Andrew asked, studying the scene.

She shook her head, wiping away tears. "It was nothing. I'm fine."

"That boy hit her," Jenny announced. "The mute one. He's *so* dangerous. I think you should tie him up again."

"Oh," Sally said, "don't do that. He just got a fright. I was checking for... for..."

"Has he anything sharp?" Andrew asked, standing between her and the boy.

"No, I don't think so. Looked like a shard of clay pipe or something."

"Huh," Andrew grunted. "What do you have, my boy? It must be important to lash out at poor Sally over it."

He held it tighter, turned his scrawny body around it.

"Are you able to get either of the Turners?" he asked Sally, appraising her closely. "Can you be quick?"

Sally nodded and made to leave the room. Andrew sat at the bench. He kept his hands down, unthreatening.

"I don't want to hurt you, son. Just don't want you hurting yourself or anyone else."

The boy stood up and started keening, a piteous cry that sounded to Sally like he was wounded. He moved his hands back and forth—the clay pipe stem dropped to the floor, forgotten.

Sally rushed out to find the Keeper.

~

James rubbed his prominent forehead and pinched the bridge of his nose. The figures on his ledger book were swimming before his eyes. In the deepening gloom, the timid light from his candle stub flickered over the jumble of dockets and receipts crowding his rolltop desk.

He paused in his book-keeping, recalling a tyrant of a schoolmaster who used to hit him for not getting sums right. It was funny, he thought, how someone's cruel act could echo on so many years later.

He shook his head, dipped his pen in the small ceramic ink pot, and began entering numbers in the book again.

"Keeper. Mr. Turner? Can you come, please?"

The door of his little office never closed right. He looked up, blinking. He recognized her by the cap of frizzy curls. It would be more proper if she tamed those better, he thought, but that was Eunice's problem.

The girl was nearly always smiling. He heard something different in her voice now.

"Sally? What's wrong?"

"Please come. The quiet boy. The one who doesn't speak. He's hit out—"

"All right," he said, cupping the candle to snuff it out with care. "I'm coming. Where is he?"

Standing up, he spotted the redness of her face, her hand against her mouth.

"Are you all right? What's happened?"

"I..." her voice caught on something. A sob. For an uncomfortable moment, he thought he might have to console her.

"Dining hall," she said, after sniffing twice.

"Go get Eunice," he said, voice gruff. "Tell her what happened. We must tie him down again."

"Oh!" she said, voice stronger. "No, don't do that. He meant nothing by it."

James stood there, astonished at being told what to do. He cast about the room, unable to look at her.

His eye settled on a small vial, stoppered with a cork, perched in one nook of his rolltop. Alongside was a hypodermic syringe, the glass tube smudged from use. James plucked it from its spot.

Opium Tincture
TABLOID BRAND™

"Very well," he said, voice cool. "Go tell Matron we'll try calming him with the medicine Dr. Cunningham recommended. Go on now."

~

Chaos reigned in the dining hall. The boy ran back and forth from one wall to another, screaming high-pitched and waving his hands erratically. Andrew had caught him twice but let him go as he trashed and bit. Jenny stood on a bench by the door, shouting directions in a voice growing ever more shrill. Some inmates had left, but others remained, enjoying the spectacle.

"Come here, you..." Andrew growled, teeth gritted.

A giddy part of him wanted to burst out laughing at the absurdity of the chase. He couldn't but feel that the boy was enjoying it.

"Andrew!" James barked from the doorway. "Hold him down, can't you?"

Eunice and Sally followed close behind him.

The boy was distracted by the new arrivals, and Andrew lunged for him. The boy squealed as if stabbed.

"I can't hold him for long, Keeper," Andrew said, his round face red with exertion. He marvelled at how strong the skinny, sinewy child was.

James said nothing, but advanced with the hypo held low. He wasn't used to its operation and some laudanum dripped to the floor. With a quick stab, he pierced the boy on the arm through his sleeve. There was an unnatural roar. For a moment, James thought he had got Andrew by mistake.

Then the boy's trashing slowed and subsided, only the whites of his eyes visible.

"Is he all right?" Sally asked, rushing to his side.

Andrew lifted the boy up, cradling him against his chest. He moaned softly against Andrew's shoulder.

"He'll be fine, just having a rest," Eunice said. "Run up and make sure his bed is made. How much did you give him, James?"

"Enough," he said, puffing. "Are you hurt, Andrew?"

"A few scrapes," Andrew replied, grinning. "Livened up my evening no end."

"Good," James nodded. "Bed early now, everyone. Nothing to worry about. Eunice..."

With a nod, his wife started ushering the others out of the hall, up to their rooms. Jenny needed some coaxing before the room was empty at last.

James sat down with a sigh on the plain bench, his hand still holding the needle, shaking.

Upstairs, Sally finished tucking the thin blanket and stiff sheet into the straw-filled mattress of the wooden frame bed. All the bed linen was stiff from over-washing, and had a faint ammonia smell. Many of the inmates were incontinent and their bedding suffered.

She stepped back as Andrew laid the thin body down, then moved in to cover him.

"Huh," Andrew said, stepping back. "Talk about a transformation. From devil to angel."

"Hush, Andrew MacDonald," she scolded, seeing Matron approach. "Matron doesn't like that kind of talk."

Andrew gave her a bland look before stepping out to allow Eunice into the little room. "I'll settle the others, Matron," he said.

Eunice nodded, sitting down on the bed next to the boy. "What a trial you are," she mused, not looking at Sally.

"He's almost like a girl, isn't he?" Sally said. "Such long hair and lashes. Pretty features..."

"Yes," she agreed with a soft chuckle. "Why don't you run down and get scissors from my room. Remember the first day he came? We didn't know if he was a boy or not. I'll cut his hair while he's gentled like this. Go on, girl."

Sally turned to leave, hand unconsciously at her red nose.

"Then you can go clean up," Eunice said over her shoulder. "Take the rest of the evening off."

~

The quiet of the deep forest amazed you—trees stretching far above your head. You tried to peer up at the sun but could only make out a faint light through the gloom. You tried to keep your eyes on closer things: the rows and rows of tall trees, the moss-covered stones and the pillars of soft yellow-green light everywhere.

Where is this? You remembered awful pain: a horrible cold coming under your skin and turning everything warm. Before that was fighting, always fighting; turning yourself inside out, trying to escape.

You spotted a path through the trees. They arched up on either side like the aisle of a cathedral. You walked along, the forest floor soft as carpet beneath your feet. You weren't walking so much as drifting along. The soft light everywhere carried you forward. It was as quiet as the cupboard you used to hide in, the closeness of the wood absorbing all sound.

One part of you struggled to run away from here, too. Although you couldn't see anyone, it felt like a rough hand had clamped down over your mouth. You could make no sound and it was difficult to turn your head. You tried turning from the path but could only move forward.

You paused from struggling to listen to a growing sound, a deep throb filling the vault of the forest. You ignored the trapped feeling and marvelled at the growing musical swell. The whole place was reverberating with it, some distant giant organ playing. Imprisonment forgotten, you felt the melody capture your heart. You needed to listen over and over.

A long time passed.

In the rapture's midst, something twitched at the edge of your vision. Far ahead: a knot of something hard to make out. The music turned dark as something impelled you toward it. Grief overcame you, to hear the tune change.

You tried twisting your head to turn back and remember the melody. Instead, the more you turned, the more discordant the music. You looked at the stately trees and saw them turning to ugly plumes of smoke. That distant thing was much closer now, and you sensed a tingling warning that it would be close when you turned your head.

Slowly, you faced forward. The music turned horrible now. No longer music, only a hard throbbing in your chest.

It was hard to see the thing in front of you. At first you thought it was the blue and white clay pipe stem, laced with minute cracks. As you gazed, fascinated, it became a giant wasp's head preening its mandibles. You stared, overcome with horror. Then it became a wolf's vicious fangs, dripping with saliva.

Every time you stared at the awful threat, it grew more intense and transformed into something else. You were afraid to look because the thing was fear itself. It was a cloud of eyes and mouths, watching and accusing. You didn't know what you had done, but it was wrong and there was no escaping it.

You had to tear away now. With every ounce of your strength, you pulled away and ran.

You ran away through a maze of corridors in a never-ending house—plain wooden walls and floors. The doors mostly opened into small rooms: cells with forlorn people huddled in the corners. You kept looking for a way out, trying different halls and doors. You sensed the thing was always near: looking for you, just at the end of the hall.

You grew ever more frantic, trying to escape, running through the hallways. It called after you: not one voice, but hundreds. It called your name: twenty or more different names. You realized you were crying, futile tears blurring your vision. And you ran and ran and ran.

~

"Da-da-da-da. Da-da-da-da. Da-da-da-da."
"Chiti WEE wiwidoo. Chiti WEE wiwidoo"
"Twit-twit-twee, twit-twit-twee."
"Conk-la-rhee-ah!"
"Pip pip pip pip pa. Pip pip pip pip pa. Pip pip pip pip pa."
"Hoo-ah-Hoo. Hooo. Hooo."
The boy's eyes opened slowly. He groaned at the effort. The dim dawn light felt as bright as midday and the teeming bird calls outside the small window were painfully loud. His head felt like it might burst if he moved.

The pang of hunger in his belly and the soiled mattress meant he had been unconscious for a long time. Yet the lassitude that stifled him meant all he could do was lie there.

~

The day being breezy and mild, James had most of the inmates out in the yard. They only permitted the most frail and elderly to lie about inside, especially on the Sabbath. Those who could were made to shuffle around the perimeter. Native, black, Irish or white, all had to parade around under James's gaze. No stopping or idling. Even if he couldn't organize any proper work for them, they were not guests.

They had built the enclosure behind the farm buildings, toward the road. For all to see.

"Keeper," Sally said, using his title as a greeting. She carried a basket full of scrubbed linen.

"Why are you working this Sunday?" he asked with a frown. Eunice and he always insisted the staff kept the day holy, although they worked all day.

Sally's eyes widened with brief guilt, then she flashed a smile. "Just some of my own and the other girls' things," she said. "Don't want to mix them up with the farm laundry."

James made an unconscious grimace. Sally's grin widened.

"He's still out," James said. "You need have no fear from anyone in this yard."

"Oh," she said. "I'm not afraid of him. More worried that he'll be all right. You gave him quite a dose."

Sally walked across the paddock to the gate near where the clothesline hung. She nodded hello to one or two of the inmates. Their only response was to watch her latch the narrow gate.

Lazing in the hay, Hugh Morash scratched his belly and stretched like a lion. A wood pigeon sighed from the rafters of the dusty barn above. Hugh had been out late carousing in Dartmouth and slipped into his cabin well past curfew.

They were pointedly loud going by his window that morning, hurrying off to church. He had stumbled out, still dressed, appearing to do the same. He had only gotten as far as the barn.

Hugh's belly rumbled, and he considered a raid on the kitchen. Still early for lunch, he mused.

Looking out over the yard, he spotted Sally marching by with her basket. That's a fine rump she has, he thought, stirring himself and carefully lowering down from his perch, his head still tender from the previous night. He ambled over to where Sally hung out clothes.

"Good morning, Sally McMahon," he said. He had his hands tucked into the little front pockets of his tatty waistcoat.

Sally gave him a quick side glance, then returned to the line. "Is it?"

"Sure it is!" he proclaimed. "Bit breezy, but the sun is shining."

"Is it morning?" she clarified. "I'm pretty sure it's past noon."

He scratched his head, considering her. He liked her wild hair, even though it was a shade too red for most people's taste. That said, there was something too smart about her pale blue eyes; the attractive dimple in her cheek was often because she smirked at him. Plus, she was tall with strong farmer's-daughter shoulders.

"I just wanted to know if you were over your tousle with that young ingrate?" he said. He thought it clever to call the inmates this. "Andrew MacDonald says you caught a right belt off of him."

"I'm fine," she said, still with her back to him.

"I don't know why we keep them all so cozy here." He looked past her down to the enclosure. "It's too nice they have it."

"What do you know about how nice they have it?" She turned on him, raising her voice. "Seems to me like you have it nice, lying about this place and only half-working."

He gave a small nod, unable to account for her quick fury. Then he remembered joking with his friends about women and their time of the month. He gave her a thin, sly smile.

"Did a bit of blood on the nose bring out the blood somewhere else?" he said. "Don't be taking it out on me."

She let go of her basket and shoved him hard on the shoulder. His jaw dropped with complete shock. She was tall, maybe taller than him, and stronger than he expected.

"You can't hit me," he insisted.

"I just did," she said, with a slight laugh. "Now bugger off while I hang out my washing."

Rubbing his shoulder, he considered hitting back. Maybe tear that blouse off her, give her a good fright. Then he thought of the strictness of the Turners.

"You just watch yourself, Sally. I'll not forget this."

She picked the last couple of clothes out of the basket, along with a few wooden pegs. With a shrug, she casually attached them to the rough rope. "I'm not afraid of you." She stared hard at him.

His upper lip quivered as emotion tore at him. He thought better of saying anything more before walking away.

Smile

Poor Farm, Cole Harbour, May 1889

"Sally? Come out here, girl."

Eunice stood in the kitchen yard, shading her eyes. It was early and cold, but the sun was bright.

"Yes, Matron?" Sally appeared at the door with a broom in her hands.

"What're you up to?"

"Just cleaning up in the kitchen. You said—"

"Never mind that. I've an errand for you. The new boy. The mute. He's been acting up something fierce. Keeping the others in the men's dorm up all night. I think if you took him on a walk, it might do him a world of good."

Sally's face betrayed sudden fear. "Is he dangerous, Matron? Andrew said he was savage. Feral. I don't know what to do with Violents. He hit me before, you know."

"Pay Andrew no mind, Sally. He's harmless since we've started giving him that medicine. It's a fine day, the start of spring. Why don't you take a picnic? Walk him out along the water. He likes cheese. Ask cook to spare something."

Sally's eyes went wide at this generosity. She tucked an errant strand of her red-blonde hair behind an ear. A broad smile dimpled one side of her freckled face. "Certainly, Matron. I'll get something now."

"Good. Mind you don't go too far. I don't want to be sending out any search parties."

~

The boy sat on the long bench at the edge of the yard. He was staring at something on the ground: a beetle with ants swarming over it. White matter seeped from its carapace.

Unsure, Sally stood before him. As instructed, she had prepared a rough picnic of hard cheddar, a flask of weak tea, and a hunk of stale bread—all Cook would spare. She had wrapped the collation in an old gingham cloth that would serve as a picnic blanket.

"Hullo there," she said. "What's your name?"

He made no reply. Although the sun shone, it was still early May and the fresh breeze coming in from the harbour had an edge to it. She liked this kind of ambivalent weather: both winter and summer, an uncertain hopefulness in the air.

"Would you like to come out on a walk with me? Matron had me put together a picnic. She can be kind, you know. If you work hard."

She said no more, waiting for his response. He would not look away from the ants parading over the dead insect. She wondered if he could hear her, never mind understand. Maybe she could leave him and go off by herself?

She looked around, noticing Matron in a far corner of the yard. She was watching them.

The breeze picked up, and he raised his head. Listening to something distant.

"I guess you don't understand. That's all right," Sally said. "Oh! I even got cheese."

She parted the tablecloth to show him the contents.

He looked quickly, face all suspicion. Then, with animal speed, he grabbed for the cheese.

Sally pulled away the parcel just in time. "Come on a walk if you want some of that."

He started looking back at the ground. With a heavy sigh, Sally reached forward and took his hand. For a second, he stared wide-eyed at her, before snatching it back.

"Come on then," she insisted. "Or I'll go without you."

She hefted the parcel of food over her shoulder and turned her back on him, taking the path worn through the field down towards the shore. She knew not to look back.

The surrounding grass was wan and yellow, worn out from a winter's weight of snow. Here and there poked the odd mayflower or dandelion.

She was as far as the gap in the split-rail fence when she spotted him from the corner of her eye. She noted the tangle of his mop of fair hair and how his donated clothes were too big. He scowled at the trees beyond the fence.

"Come on," called Sally. "I don't bite." She crossed the gap in the fence, humming to herself.

The way through the woods was uneven; the ground all roots, mossy stones and pine needles. Birds congregated in the branches overhead, calling back and forth. Some maples already sported bright russet clusters of blossoms.

Sally spied a fat robin picking at something in the tangle of roots beneath a large hemlock. She got near before it flew off, twittering its annoyance.

He was still behind her, quiet as a ghost.

"Come on, you," she called back. "We only have a couple of hours, then Matron wants us back."

A lance of light broke through the trees surrounding a clearing. Sally smiled as she made for it. "We don't want to spend the entire time in the gloomy old woods, do we?

It's not far to where Stink Brook meets the estuary. There's a quiet cove beyond."

She stepped past the shaft of sunlight and heard a crunch. Looking down, she noticed a smashed shell, the other half nearby.

"Come see," she called. "That's why the robin was hopping about. Her chicks have hatched."

Sally lifted the intact half shell, a quarter the size of a hen's egg. He crept forward to peer at the delicate cyan colour.

"Pretty, isn't it," she said. "Here. Take it."

He looked at her, mouth half-open. She slowly put the shell piece back on the ground.

"You can look at it. If you want."

He considered for a long time, rocking back and forth and making a low moaning sound.

"That's all right. You don't have to if you don't want to. Look over there. Fiddleheads!"

At the edge of the sunny spot sprouted a small cluster of translucent yellow-green ferns. As Sally went to study them, he picked up the shell and crunched it. He looked at her, the broken delicate thing in his hands.

"Oh," she said. "Too bad. Not to worry. I think we'll leave the fiddleheads, though. Another week or two, maybe we can come back for them."

He stared at her, as if stunned by what she had said.

She cocked her head to one side. "You hear, don't you?" she marvelled. "That's good."

She slowed the flow of her words, speaking more deliberately. "We don't have to pick these yet." She pointed at the cluster of ferns. "But we'll come back in two weeks and they'll be stronger. A lot more, too, I should think. Cook can stew them up. They're right tasty."

He made no response, just kept looking at her.

"Well then," Sally said. "Shall we keep on? I expect that mother robin wants to get back up to her chicks and we're putting her off."

She took a deep breath and walked on, her mind on things other than her strange companion. When she heard the susurration of Stink Brook, she looked back.

Shading her eyes, she wrinkled her nose as she scanned behind her. No sign of him. She swore aloud. Would she get in trouble if he ran off? She should have pointed that out to Matron earlier. She thought of search parties and all the bother there would be.

She sighed and took a few steps back when she heard a crashing through the undergrowth. He squealed with delight, running past her and into the fast-moving stream ahead.

Sally cursed inwardly, watching him hop up and down, splashing at the surface of the water. "Oh, no! You're soaked through. Come out of there."

She stood at the edge of the rivulet. The smell wasn't so strong down this far. The effluent from the farm made its way out to the sea and could be pungent, depending on the residents' activities.

Sally suddenly burst out in delighted laughter. He was standing in the middle of the creek, splashing and calling out. On his face was a broad smile. She had never seen a face so transformed.

At the brook's edge, a large gnarled burl protruded from a tree trunk. Sally sat against the giant wart of wood, watching him splash. There was no gain in taking him away from such obvious pleasure. She spread the gingham cloth out on the mossy ground, leaving the food and drink in the middle. Humming to herself again, she arranged portions for both of them.

So absorbed with her task, she shrieked when he stood over her, dripping dirty water all over the blanket. He was moaning inaudibly, trying to mimic the first notes of the tune she was singing. At first, it sounded like mockery.

"Stewart! What are you doing? I mean—"

She covered her mouth. She hadn't meant to call him that. Something convulsed in her, an unwanted memory. She swallowed and shook her head.

"Well, why not give you that name?" she reasoned aloud, standing and taking his shirt off. He did not resist.

"What if you catch a chill, Stewart?" There. She said it again. She took off her shawl and draped it around his thin shoulders. She inhaled sharply at the sight of his pigeon chest. His ribs plainly visible. Scars covered his pale skin. She drew back, wondering what to do.

"I'll take off those trousers," she said. "But we have to wrap you in the gingham to dry off proper. You can have this." She picked up the cheese and put it on a nearby stone. "If you sit quiet on that rock."

He allowed her to remove his soaked pants, which she laid out on a low branch to dry. She placed their food on the rock beside him and bent to gather up the tablecloth.

"Oh, you!" she scolded. She had turned her back. He was already into the hard cheddar, gnawing at it. He took fright at her tone and stood, dropping cheese and shawl. He shrieked at her, hair and wretched naked body still drenched.

"Shush, now. Shush. No need to get as upset as all that. Here." She picked up the cheese. "It's alright. You can have it. It's fine, Stewart."

His breath kept coming in terrified fits, but he took it from her.

"All right. Now I'll put the cloth on you. To dry you off."

When she came close, he made to bolt. She drew back, remembering a song from home.

Horo hi rithill a bha ho
Ho hi rithill a bha ho

She sang in a low tone, not wanting to frighten him.

He chewed at the cheese, looking back at the stream. As gently as possible, she gathered the rough cloth and surrounded him with it. His breathing was even now, as she kept singing the same two lines.

It wasn't even proper Gaelic, that part of the song. When she was small, listening to her grandmother, she wondered what the actual words might have been. Someone must have forgotten and put those place words in. Maybe they thought they could fix it up later. Only the nonsense remained.

With a sigh, she sat beside him on the uncomfortable rock. The bread and flask she placed on the earth. He was still looking at the water.

"I never knew you liked songs, Stewart. I've lots of them, if you don't mind me singing." She laughed. "I hope you don't mind me calling you Stewart. He was someone special."

She paused, the brook murmuring to itself in the silence. The sun made an appearance through the pine trees. She unscrewed the little flask and filled the tin cup with lukewarm tea. "Not too bad here, I suppose. Would have been nicer down by the water. We'd get the full of the sunshine. Maybe next time. Oh! I should introduce myself properly. My name's Sally McMahon."

She held out her hand to him. He made no response. She held it out for a while, shrugged, then took a drink of tea.

"Not to worry," she continued. "I'm from Baddeck originally. Up in Cape Breton. The lake is nice there. McMahon sounds like Micmac, doesn't it? There are plenty of Indians up there, too. They have their language and we have ours. Funny, isn't it? I've heard there are a few around here, but they keep to themselves. A good few in the farm, too. Though they call themselves half-breeds."

He interrupted her chatter with a loud belch. He knocked over the little cup from where she had placed it between them.

"Hey!" said Sally, careful to talk in a low tone. "Well, there goes the tea. Maybe you prefer singing to talking?"

She picked up the cup, wiping it off. The tea tasted bitter anyway.

"Oh dear, don't do that."

He kept on belching, sometimes chortling aloud. Sally sighed. What harm was it, really? They would scold him enough at the farm for it. At least he was smiling again. Then he burped so loudly, he brought back up some cheese. He happily picked the spittle-sodden mess from his gaping mouth, twiddling it with glee.

"All right," Sally said. "That is not a nice thing to do. Why don't you have a drink of tea to wash down that cheese? There's bread too."

He laughed again, smiling at her. Re-swallowing the cheese, he took the proffered flask. Some of it dribbled down his chin as he loudly quaffed it down. Sally shook her head.

"That's good, I suppose." She retrieved the flask, offering some bread. "Well, I think this is lovely, Stewart. I'll sing a song or two and you and your clothes will dry off. Promise you won't spit up any more food or jump in the water?"

His excited laughter was the only response.

~

Homespun Pants	(Union)	1 75/100	per pair		
" "	(All wool)	2 25/	"	"	"
Moleskine Vests	(Union)	100/	"	"	"
Moleskine "	(All wool)	135/	"	"	"
Drawers	(Union)	450/	"	"	"
"	(Scarlet wool)	800/	"	"	"
"	(Heavy wool, Ribbed)	1200/	"	"	"
"	(Grey, Ribbed)	600/	"	"	"

Eunice whispered the words from the handwritten invoice as she scribbled into the ledger, taking stock of new items. The afternoon light only provided a dim gloom and there was no window.

Sally bustled in, humming to herself. She held the damp tablecloth in her arms. "Oh, Matron!" she exclaimed. "I didn't know you were in here."

Eunice looked up, tired eyes widening to relieve them. She rubbed her lined forehead. "You're back, I see. Took longer than I expected. How did you fare?"

"It was fine," Sally said guardedly. "Stewart. I mean the patient. He loves music. And so do I. So—"

"Stewart? How do you know his name?" Eunice scrutinized Sally now, as if she were an erroneous figure in her notebook.

"I don't. I...I just gave him that name. It helped, you know. Taking him for a walk like that. He enjoyed it."

"Hmm," said Eunice, taking the damp bundle from her. "This should probably go to the wash. I'm glad you enjoyed yourself taking him out there. Just don't forget what a handful he can be. I expect someone, a parent, took him on a lengthy walk in the woods once. Only left him. That's why he ended up here."

Sally nodded, eyes downcast.

"Anyway," Eunice said, in a kinder tone. "It's good you could calm 'Stewart'. Go on, let's take this to the laundry pile. I can't see my way around here anymore."

Song

Poor Farm, Cole Harbour

The sewing room was on the second floor of the Centre Wing. Although it was not yet dark, the room filled with honey light from a paraffin lamp.

Sally drowsed a little, lulled by the faint burnt smell of the oil and the repetitive work of darning a piece of calico. Her eyes closed for a few long moments and she slumped forward. She jerked her head up, snapped out of her dozing.

Eunice gave her a sharp look, glancing up from her pedal-driven sewing machine occupying a corner of the room. It was a gleaming, black-and-gold painted beast with "Singer" embossed in large letters on one side. "Don't be falling asleep, girl," she said. "We still have to get some of these to bed later."

Jenny and some of the other mostly sane inmates could work as seamstresses. Eunice even had local farm wives send in clothes for repair and charged them for it; although not overmuch. To Eunice's mind, the girls should be glad of the work. It was far better than toiling out in the fields with the saner men. These days they often came back filthy with sweat and soil from clearing boulders in the field that needed heavy reclamation.

"Sorry, Matron," Sally said. "I'm not that tired, really. A bit distracted, maybe."

"Why don't you sing us something? You're always humming."

"Oh, no," Sally said, freckled cheeks a-blush. "I can't sing."

"*On no, Ma'am. I can't sing,*" Jenny mocked her, making a face. "You're always singing."

"Go on," Eunice said. "It'll help us work. Nothing too bawdy, mind you. Remember, this is a Christian institution."

Her eyes strayed to the simple crucifix on the wall that watched over their labours.

"It will have to be a tragic one, so," she said, smiling. "My Gran was great for those. Does anyone know 'The Silvery Tide'?"

Shaking of heads and murmurings of "No."

"Very well. Prepare yourselves. It's a bit of a long one."

There was no objection while Sally composed herself, trying to remember how it went. Settling back into the sewing, she sang.

The clarity of her voice surprised them. Eunice found herself timing the down-press of the machine's pedal to the rhythm of the tune. Her spool was running low, but she was loath to stop and interfere with the girl's performance.

> It's of a lovely creature lived down by the seaside,
> So lovely form and feature,
> > she was called the village bride,
> There was a young sea captain
> > who oft came her to see,
> So true she proved to Henery, all on the raging main.
>
> All in young Henery's absence
> > a nobleman there came,
> A-courting lovely Mary, but she refused the same,
> "Your vows they're vain while o'er the main

there's one I love," she cried,
    "It's Henery I love dearly, I'll die by his sweet side."

One morning as this nobleman
    went out to take the air,
Down by this rolling ocean he met this lady fair,
"Now," said this wretched nobleman,
    "consent to be my bride
Or I'll send your body floating far on the silvery tide."

"Young Henery..." Sally paused, recollecting the next line.

"I *like* this one," Jenny said to the girl beside her. "Imagine some rich man having his way with you and throwing you out to sea. Sorry, Matron."

"I remember now," Sally said, continuing before Matron could censure her.

"Young Henery I love dearly,
    my vows I can never break,
All in young Henery's absence,
    I'll die for his sweet sake,"
With a handkerchief he bound her hands
    and plunged her over the side,
And swiftly she went floating
    down on the silvery tide.

About six weeks after this,
    young Henery came from sea,
Expecting to see Mary and appoint the wedding day,
"I fear your true love's murdered,"
    her agèd parents cried,
"For she's proved her own destruction
    down by the silvery tide."

> As young Henery on his bed of down,
>> he could not take his rest,
> The thoughts of murdered Mary
>> disturbed his aching breast,
> He dreamed that he was walking
>> far down by the ocean side
> And saw his true love floating
>> down on the silvery tide.

"Is it her ghost?" Jenny interrupted again.

"Shush," Eunice said, despite herself. "Let her finish the song. It's lovely."

Sally blushed. Her voice wavered a little as she continued, self-conscious. Once she got caught up in the melody again, it transported her to the tragedy and she forgot the stuffy room.

> He knew that it was Mary by
>> his own ring on her hand,
> When he unbound the handkerchief
>> and brought her in to stand,
> The name of this base murderer
>> there enveloped he spied,
> As she to and fro went floating
>> down on the silvery tide.

> This nobleman was taken, the gallows was his doom
> For murdering lovely Mary,
>> who scarce was in her bloom,
> Young Henery was distracted, until the day he died,
> And his last words were for Mary,
>> who died on the silvery tide.

Sally felt pleased with the hush that settled when she finished. As a child, everyone had to sing a song during winter evenings stuck inside and this was hers. Her family often praised her for it, even her formidable grandmother, herself a fine singer.

For once, Jenny had nothing to say. She snuck a glance at Matron, who was looking past her, out to the hall.

"Dow ah the sibbery tide," Stewart sang. "Dow ah the sibbery tide."

He stood at the door, wraith-like. His eyes were cast to the floor, like a schoolboy giving a recitation.

"My goodness," Eunice exclaimed. "You've made him speak!"

"That's good, Stewart," Sally said, beaming at the youth. "Keep singing!"

He stopped, embarrassed. Then ran away down the hall.

"Matron, may I go after him? See if I can get him to sing again."

"By all means," she said, her astonishment plain. "Doctor said he couldn't speak at all."

"Thanks, Matron. I'll see if I can get him to say more."

"It was like an angel," Jenny said, caught up in the excitement. "Wonder if it's some kind of miracle, Matron?"

"Perhaps," Eunice replied, watching Sally depart. Shaking her head, she murmured, "Might be a miracle this farm needs."

Sally caught up with Stewart by the stairs.

"Stewart? Did you really sing in there?"

He didn't reply, face as passive as ever. She went to touch his shoulder before withdrawing her hand. He reminded her of a sleepwalker and she knew how dangerous it was to wake them.

She sat down on the step beside him and spoke in a soothing voice. "'Down on the silvery tide'? You liked that song, didn't you? I wonder why you liked it so much."

"Dow ah the sibbery tide..."

His whisper was as gentle as a distant wood pigeon. He looked at her directly, large hazel eyes intense, willing her to understand.

"That's lovely, Stewart," she said, wondering at the directness of his gaze. "Do you want to go there? Down to the seaside? I can go back and ask Matron. She said part of my job is to help... patients."

The side of his mouth twitched—the slightest of smiles.

"Stay there. It's worth a try. I'm sick of sewing and mending, anyway."

He wandered downstairs while she rushed back to get permission.

"Hey," she called after him, breathless. "You're supposed to wait for me! We caught Matron in a good mood and can go. Not too long. Have to be back by curfew."

She unlocked the front door with the key Matron had loaned her. Outside, bats swooped back and forth in the gloom, feasting on midges. She looked up at the clear sky, marvelling at how the slight creatures always seemed to pass at the edge of her vision.

"See all the bats out tonight?" she said, picking up her pace to match his. "I don't mind them. Although I know girls terrified they'll pitch in your hair. Doesn't seem likely, they fly so well in the dark. Nobody knows how they do it."

They were by the gate now. He stood silent while she fumbled with the lock. Matron was very careful who got the key.

"A cluster of them would roost in our neighbours' barn. In the day, they made funny squealing sounds as they hung upside down, close together. Their eyes closed tight. Blind—"

With a whoop, he was past her, through the gate and down the path to the shoreline.

"Stewart," she cried. "Be careful! Wait for me."

~

You run and run. Run barefoot through the bramble, laughing all the while. You rush through the woods. Away, away, away. No one telling you what to do, where to go— telling you all those things that make no sense. None of the yelling. No faces. Those faces that are so hard to look at, you can't tell if it is your own face you are looking at.

She is different, though. Her face isn't so hard to look at. But that isn't enough reason not to enjoy being free. You hear her calls from behind you, but you don't stop.

You stumble along the rocks, down to the shore. Thin, cool mist fills the air. You like it, even though you feel cold. Your feet sting from the sharp stones by the water's edge, so you run through the long sea grass. Down along the estuary. Strange birds cry out at you, but you keep running. You slip and fall but get up just as quick.

It turns to night but you can still see everywhere, the moon above and only a few clouds. The shining moon cuts a path through the sea—the silvery shore. The shouting of the waves takes over everything. You need to get away from the noise.

You keep running, feet making a nice sucking sound as you careen along the flat sand. The sea still shouts, but not so loud here. You pause, panting from the exertion. You aren't locked up anymore. No one telling you to stand there, tying you to the chair when you don't eat, hitting you without telling you why.

"Stewart? Where are you? Come back, you little bugger..."

Her voice sounds strange, not like when she sings. She is up on the sea grass, calling out. The wind had picked up and rolled the mist away. You can see her in the rising moonlight. If you wait, maybe she will go away. Like before.

Part of you doesn't like the change, leaving the farm routine behind. Then you think of being locked up. You hate that. You slip further down the shore. Away further.

"Stewart," she cries out. "Do you want me to sing again?"

She begins singing but her voice catches on "swiftly she went floating down on the silvery tide." *Why would she do that?* You want to hear the rest of the song then and wander over to where she sits.

The moon is up now and you can see her holding her head in her hands. Instead of singing, she weeps; rebuking herself over and over.

You cock your head to one side, puzzled. Why wouldn't she be happy to be down here? You touch her shoulder.

She startles back, staring at you. Then there are more tears and "Oh, Stewart!" and "You're all right!"

It isn't long before you've had enough of *that*! You squeeze her arm and grit your teeth until she stops.

"What is it?" she asks, wiping her eyes. "What do you want?"

You hate this. You have to say something. It takes a while to make the sounds right. She listens silently on the low hump of sand grass, face moon pale.

"*Awn ah the sibbery tide...*"

She understands then. You rock back and forth with delight as she sings it all for you. The whole thing. Again.

Buggy

Poor Farm, Cole Harbour, April, 1890

James took his time getting over to the well. His back ached, and he wanted to keep himself clean.

He put down the bucket and turned, surveying the morning. The three principal buildings of the poor farm had their backs turned to him: white-washed shingles, curtainless windows and pitched roofs. It was an odd arrangement, each two-story dormitory connected by a short hallway to the Centre Wing, where the kitchen and their rooms were. The effect was not of an institution but of a family farm where they built the next generation's houses right on top of each other.

Several men idled in the yard. No sign of Andrew or Hugh. James sighed.

He stared out to the sea beyond. He could make out the specks of a pair of dories. They were coming in now, the day's work done.

Reminded of his task, he lifted the wooden bucket by its rough rope handle and hurried over to the well. Brambles surrounded the sunk stone circle. Teeming tadpoles wriggled away as he dipped the bucket in. He tipped some water back, listening to the lapping sound. Too much and he might slop it all over his pants. Besides, he reflected, his back was too stiff for carrying. Stevie would make do with half a bucket.

A reptilian eye blinked, followed by a flash of blood red and sulphur yellow. The painted turtle slipped into the water, unhappy with his presence.

He trudged along the ridge to the new stable, grudgingly paid for by Council. James would have preferred more dormitory buildings but was told to wait. He put the bucket down by the horse.

"Here you go, Stevie. Hope this will keep you until we get to the Squire's. Not that far."

The horse, nose deep in the bucket, paid no attention. He was mostly meek now, after being caught and fixed.

"Sometimes I think you say more to that horse than to me."

He studied Eunice, mild surprise in his eyes. She was dressed for going out: best black frock and the hat with a small matching veil. "Do I?"

"I want you to take me into Dartmouth."

"I'm only going as far as your Bissett's. My monthly report." He tapped the wad of papers in his waistcoat pocket.

"I know that. I want to see Sophia, besides. We can go on to town. *The Daily Echo* has an office on Portland Street."

"The what? I have to be back... for..."

"For what? You're the Keeper, James. Everything can wait until this afternoon. I'll be in the buggy while you get Stevie ready."

The horse gave him a meaningful look while he readied the harness and bridle. Keeping his frustration tamped down, he said nothing until he had the traces set right, opened the gate and laboriously climbed up beside his wife.

"We must get him oats at Bissett's," he muttered as they creaked out of the little stable yard.

"That's fine," she said. "I expect we won't be there long."

"You don't have post for them?"

George, being a councilman, received and held mail for everyone around. Hearing no reply, he gave Stevie a quick glance, then stared hard at the road ahead. The horse didn't need much direction; he knew the way.

"Aren't you going to ask me?" she said, once the farm buildings passed from view.

"Ask you?"

"Oh, for heaven's sake, James. Don't you want to know *why* I'm going into the newspaper?"

"Expect I'll read it soon enough."

"The boy," she said, after making a cross sound. "What does Sally call him? Stewart. You heard what happened?"

"I heard we nearly lost an inmate to the sea."

"Yes. I reprimanded her about that. But if it weren't for her, he might not have come back. Besides, even you can see how he's improving with her care. He was wild as a savage before. To speak, even to sing!"

James said nothing. His wife often mistook his silence for denseness.

"Don't you see? We need something like this. Something to improve our reputation. This inspector that's coming from the Overseers. What's his name?"

"Emmett Forrestall."

"I don't know what political twists and turns George has got mixed up in, but there have been more and more questions about the running of the farm. You lending out some of them to Abbot—"

"Our son needed help mending his barn."

"All the same, it looked bad."

"We have to lend out Stevie here to any farm around but can't do it with the few inmates who can work."

She made a face at the bitterness in his voice. "What do you expect? They don't know how hard it is to run the place. Never enough money, and we get the absolute dregs most of the time. That's why this boy could be important for us. Distract this Forrestall with some good news. We *are* supposed to be helping them improve."

"We are?"

She said nothing, fixing her gaze on the trees rolling by. The carriage wobbled on its suspension. Like many things they had, it was second-hand and needed mending. George Bissett liked to point this out to her every time they alighted in his yard.

"They might not even be interested," Eunice mused, almost to herself. "Although some of the scandalous trash they print there. Makes you wonder."

"Not sure it's a good idea. Drawing attention."

"Oh, you always think that. Everyone needs a good news story, once in a while. It was hard enough convincing them to let us have this farm. Now we're making something of it. Why not have a bit of..." She paused, unable to come to the right word.

"Problem is," he rumbled, interrupting her for once. "They keep sending more. We're already full."

"They must build more dormitories. Get us more staff. Lord knows we're stretched to the maximum as it is. Times are hard and there are always people who can't make their way. They send them to us, expecting them to work. They can't work. How many do we confine to the beds these days? Eleven, isn't it? You put them clearing fields or sewing when the time comes, but how many are good enough at it? The women I have sewing or cleaning..."

She shook her head, images of some of their more pitiful charges floating there. "We don't have to be a *poor* farm, James. We could make a better go of it."

James bowed his head. There was no changing her mind, and it was easier to lapse into silence than get browbeaten.

He shifted uneasily on the hard wooden seat of the carriage. By his estimation, it was seven miles from Bissett's to Dartmouth and his tail-end would be numb by the time they got there. One thing he was fairly sure of, that boy was going to be trouble.

He shook the reins to hurry Stevie forward. The horse paid him no mind.

Violents' room

Poor Farm, Cole Harbour

This is the room for Violents. It has no window. You can't see the sea. It is plain and dark—pine wood walls and floor. A box with an iron-frame spring bed, and a bucket.

The smell is potent near the bucket. It sits in one corner like a guard. So you have to hold on to the urge to go for a long time. You need to wait a really long time!

It can be an agreeable feeling, the way it builds and builds inside. When you can't hold on any longer, you rush over there to do it and quick back again.

You must not do it in the bed. The first time you did, Andrew came in and shouted at you. He made you stand by the bucket and rushed back with clothes and a wash-basin of freezing water. You hate clothes. They scratch and itch and get covered in your own soil. Why does everyone wear them? Even when it is cold out, there is a pleasant sting on your skin.

They have sent you to the room a few times now. This time, there was no reason. Just sent here. And for a long time. *How long?* It's hard to know.

The little door in the door opened sometimes and a pair of eyes stared at you. It is curious when eyes are on their own like that. After seeing no-one for a long time and then eyes, you can read them. You see words like "Cruel", "Bored" and "Tired". When the rest of the features appear, when the door opens and they look in, you can't read anymore. Too much, all at once. Like not having a finger under the word when reading.

No one here knows you can read or how you figured it out.

How long will they leave you here this time? You screw your eyes tight, remembering that little cocoon on a bush in your family's yard. What had it been before that? Mother showed you. The cocoon's brown casing was horrible and alien, but the butterfly crawled out the bottom, wings shining like coloured glass. Was that why they trapped you in here? But every time you came out, you were always the same.

You open your eyes. Back in the room again. You wonder how you could see when there's no window.

You realize it's not a perfect box. There are chinks in the pine wall. Light seeps in under the door. Sometimes you crouch there and peer at feet going back and forth. You know when it is night as nobody is around.

Sometimes you make a howling noise but don't really try too hard. You dislike when they come, pushing a tray of food through the hatch.

One or two of them try to talk or yell at you. Then the old problem again. This thing they do—the quick words back and forth. Talking. You have watched speaking: like watching a flock of birds roll and shift in unison across the sky. A crucial part of it was to tell someone what to do: to keep insisting "*You*", "*You*" and "*You*". You puzzle over this in silence and they give up and leave. You are alone in the room again.

You found a way through this. You walked. One end of the room to the other, avoiding that odorous corner. Walk. Back and forth, singing. Doesn't matter what, so long as you sang. There's no-one to stop you singing here. They don't like it when you sing outside. Even though your singing is lovely.

There might not be any words, but the sounds have their own colours. A deep sound was a brown or a black. A high moan or squeal was a yellow-green. Remember that time in the woods when the sun speared through the green roof of leaves? This was one picture you sang as you went back and forth between low moans and high-pitched shrieks. Nobody stopped you.

But you get tired. Sitting down on the creaky bed, you look around at the walls with those dirty words scratched into them. You miss proper colours: the silver blue of the sea and the sky. The grey black stones on the beach. You make a sad sound, like the crunching of stones by the enormous mouth of the sea. Thinking about it is not the same as being out there, being stuck in this wooden box of a room.

How long have they kept you here? Forever and forever, or maybe only a day. Your head often goes empty of memories. Did you use them all up? You sit up in a panic.

There is darkness outside. It must be night. You rub your eyes. Was there anhything else happy to think about?

You remember the ride in the cart with the farmer. The swaying motion thrilled you, and you danced your hands up and down to balance the excitement of it. He caught you trying to steal cheese from his pantry. It had been so long since you had cheese. That was the first time you ran. You had been in the woods a long time and the hunger was so strong.

He yelled at you as if you were a wild dog. He came closer, stick in hand, then stopped when he saw you up close. You got trapped there in that kitchen, in that corner. He said shocked things, putting down his stick. He called for someone, then said soothing things. You couldn't understand, but he let you eat the cheese.

An old woman came. She spoke in a high off-pitch tone, making you cover your ears and yell. They drew back, looking at each other.

"What'll we do, mother?" the farmer said.

"I don't know. Take him to the doctor. Or the police. Look at the state of his clothes. And his leg! It's all festering."

You were used to the sore leg. The wolf got you as you scrambled up a tree. It took a long time for it to leave you alone.

The mother left, her mouth wide open. She came back with old pants. You fought with him for a long time before he got them on you. It was sore there, and the cheese had given you back some strength. The farmer had to tie your hands to the table legs. Even then you kicked and yelled. His eyes kept rolling about and he repeated, "Lord, Oh Lord!"

He put a dog collar on your neck and brought you out to his cart. You were meek then, hating the pants, but they were on now. The mother had tried to wash you and you had bitten her arm. She stood by the farm door, holding it.

"Preserve us, Sidney! He's got the devil in him."

You loved the ride away from there. It was still a wonderful memory. The motion of the wheels was something you could anticipate, but sometimes it varied. It was like the laughing sounds of a stream and you giggled along with its delight. The best part was jigging your hands back and forth, trying to match its rhythm.

He took you to the town. You disliked being near so many buildings and people. You hated the terrible jumble of sound and smell and light. You curled into a corner of the cart when he pulled into a dusty yard. He tried to get you out but you wouldn't go. Couldn't he keep going? Leave this awful place?

He gave up on wheedling and left you there for a long while. You were thinking of escape when he returned. This time with a constable.

The constable took off his helmet and stroked his big moustache. "Ain't that something, Sidney?"

"Does anyone know who he might be? Anyone lost a boy?"

The constable shook his head, staring at you.

"Be careful," Sidney said. "He bit my Missus."

"Not sure if we can take him in," the constable said. "He's a child. What about the poor farm? I'll go out with you."

The men spoke some more. Eventually, the constable climbed up next to the farmer and they left with you. You didn't jig so much this time as the cart creaked along. The horse was getting tired and wasn't going as fast.

That was how you came to the farm.

The door opens. It is Andrew. He pushes the door open and steps back. The morning light floods the room. You are blind for a while.

"All right, Stewart, m'boy," Andrew calls. "C'mon out now. They reckon the diphtheria is gone from the rooms."

Slowly, you get up from the bed and leave the Violents' room.

The Daily Echo

SINGS WITH AN ANGEL'S VOICE
- Iris Dowden
Cole Harbour, Apr. 27 —

At a recent visit to The Cole Harbour County Poor Farm, we were received by Matron Eunice Turner and her husband, Keeper James Turner. They have been running the farm for several years in this remote spot near the shore. They informed us that many cases end up here: the poor who do not work and the harmlessly insane.

Amid this darkness, the Matron introduced us to a minor miracle. A mute boy, found living rough in the woods around Musquodoboit, was discovered to sing "with an angel's voice". "We thought him dumb at first and a demon to all. Through his care at the farm, he shows he can sing many songs, sometimes after only hearing them once."

Other staff at the farm informed us that the boy will now sing a phrase when he wishes for something. He might even sing *The Jug of Punch* if he desires a drink. I am assured this Troubadour only ever gets water or, as a special treat, milk! The matron begs us to include the detail that without the Poor

Farm, these misfortunate souls are left to the whims of fate.

A birdie sat on an ivy bunch,
And the song he sang
was a jug o' punch.

Uncle Tom's Cabin

Poor Farm, Cole Harbour, May 1890

Walking from the stables, Emmett sniffed at his first sight of the poor farm. Of all the things he hated about farms, he despised their smell the most. His abiding memory of his father's family farm in Ireland was the repulsive odour of pigs. He remembered the beasts terrifying him as they screamed pitifully from some sty.

Emmett picked his way down to what looked like the front door of the Central Wing and knocked. He waited, eyeing the high grass growing to the door. The meagre lawn ended with a line of nearby apple trees, twisted from the harsh wind off the sea. A flagless flagpole stood off to one side.

He was considering trying to gain entrance through the empty enclosure around the back when the door opened.

"Oh," Eunice said, wiping her hands and laughing nervously. "You'll be Mr. Forrestall. We didn't expect you 'til later. We're just preparing lunch."

"Thank you," Emmett said, wondering at her old-fashioned black gown. "I'm from the Overseers."

"Of course. Forgive me! I'm Eunice Turner, Matron of the farm. Please come in."

Emmett followed her into the narrow hall. He noticed the plain, straw-yellow wallpaper: warped and creased; it reminded Emmett of aged foolscap.

"We're all thrilled to have a visitor, Mr. Forrestall," Eunice said. "Just through this way."

He barely registered the false enthusiasm in her voice before being assailed by the sight before him. His first thought was of one of the black and white minstrel shows he had seen as a teenager.

"I didn't expect 'Uncle Tom's Cabin'," he murmured.

Eunice narrowed her eyes, assessing him. "We have a lot of elderly black men. Some of our best workers. We take all kinds here."

Lined, weary faces stared back at him. The blankness of their gazes unnerved Emmett. Others looked down or into the distance, drool or remnants of food on their chins. Some staff busied about, chivying them through their meal.

Emmett watched them with dismay until Eunice brought him to a livelier table in the corner, where a few children sat. "And these are the little ones," she announced. "Children! Say hello to Mr. Forrestall."

They greeted him in raucous unison. He noticed one as young as six or seven.

"Do they get schooling?"

"Some," she said, voice prim. "We get the pastor regularly for their Sunday School. And this…" Her tone changed as she gestured toward a taller boy, sitting apart from the others. "This is Stewart. Our singing star!"

"Singing st-st-star?" Emmett echoed, incredulous.

"Yes. He's been in *The Daily Echo* and everything. Sally! Come and meet Mr. Forrestall."

"Please, call me Emmett," he mumbled, watching Sally get up from helping an elderly Mi'kmaq woman with long white hair. A few of the residents gathered near, intrigued by the distraction.

"Emmett," Eunice confirmed, pleased. "Sally, this is Mr. Forrestall. From the Overseers. Tell him about Stewart."

One side of Sally's mouth turned up in a wry smile. "What would you like me to tell?" she asked.

Eunice frowned, giving her a look. One child dared to giggle.

"He don't talk," a young Black man said. "He sure can sing, though."

"Thank you, Sky," Sally said. "Stewart never spoke when he came. We thought he was mute. One day, I took him out for a walk. I suppose I was humming some song or other. Next I knew, he was singing along."

"He's sung for me too," Sky added, eager to help. "He's good."

Emmett swallowed, trying to ignore Sky's enormous deformed lower lip. He tried to look at Sally instead, but found himself also dumbfounded by the young woman. His mind raced, at a loss of what to say next.

"Well," Eunice said. "I'll leave you get acquainted while I find the Keeper: my husband, James. I expect he's out somewhere mending something."

"Oh yes," Sky said, self-consciously covering his lower lip with his hand. "Do you know 'Brown Girl'? I sang that out in the yard one day. Next thing he was coming out with the line 'With diamonds and jewels I'll deck my brown girl'. Mind you, he didn't but repeat that last line."

Emmett kept nodding, unsure of what to say next. Stewart sat motionless, ignoring everyone.

Emmett looked back to Sky, trying not to stare at his lip. "And you?" he asked. "Were you mute as well?"

"Oh Lord," the young man laughed. "I'm sure there's many would wish that."

"Sky here has lots of stories," Sally said. "He's even been to Maine and New Brunswick with the travelling circus."

Sky made a face. Emmett noted the sadness in his eyes.

"I don't like to talk about then," he said. "Folks up there were mean, on account of my mouth. My proper name's Ned. Ned Beals. They call me Sky because I'm so open and nice! I used to sell at the market down in Alderney. Lots of people liked my baskets. I'd sing too. Folks liked it. Maybe I got too popular. Who knows? Gang of ruffians took a dislike to me. They were always tormenting me. One day I throw a rock to get them to leave me alone. Broke a shop window. Anyway. Ended me up here."

The man's story gave Emmett a chance to recover himself.

As he watched Stewart, a thought formed in Emmett's mind. *An opportunity.* "Can he sing now?" he asked, nodding down at Stewart.

Sally pursed her lips. "He's not a parrot," she said, one hand on her hip. Emmett blinked, surprised by her defiant tone.

"But he'll sometimes sing a line or two," she continued. "When he wants a thing. It might have a meaning connected to what he wants. Maybe Sky had something shiny that day and that's why he sang about jewels."

"Remarkable," Emmett breathed. He wasn't sure he meant Stewart or Sally. "I would like to—"

"Lunch's over," a gruff voice called from the door.

Sky and a few others backed away. James trudged in, followed by Eunice.

"Finish up now, everyone," Eunice called from behind. "Mr. Forrestall can't waste his entire day idling about."

"Sally," James said, ignoring Emmett. "Help get them out, won't you?"

Sally inclined her head, then began shooing the children out of the room.

"Wait!" Emmett said. "I'd like to...find out more. Interview him, I mean."

James stared at Emmett, blue eyes cold.

"Please excuse my husband," Eunice said, her voice and smile placatory. "He always wants to keep this place running smooth. Routine is important, and it's time for them to go outside."

She gave a curt nod to Sally, who took the message and started shepherding everyone out. Stewart followed the others, covering his mouth with one hand, mimicking Sky, who had already vanished.

"I'm sure we can arrange...something," Eunice continued. "Emmett. This is James."

"James Turner," James said, voice low enough to be a growl. "Keeper."

"Pleasure to meet you," Emmett said, putting out his hand. "Forrestall. Emmett. I'm the Assessor with the Overseers."

James's expression softened somewhat as he shook Emmett's hand. An awkward silence ensued as they watched Sally and the other staff moving inmates from the room. The old, infirm and curious ones took their time, some hoping to hear a nugget to share outside. Emmett wavered between waiting on the old man to say something and trying to think of a pleasantry. Eunice stood between them, suddenly quiet, lips clenched in an unconscious grimace.

In the interval, Emmett formed a plan.

"Would you like to come through to our office?" Eunice said, breaking the silence when they were the only ones remaining.

"No, no. Here is fine," Emmett said. "I'll get right down to it, Mr. and Mrs. Turner. There have been complaints to Council. About the running of the farm—"

"Well, I find that very unfair," Eunice exclaimed. "We always keep very accurate accounts. Don't we, James? And you can see how happy they are here. We work them hard, too."

"That's just the thing," Emmett said, raising a hand. "There have been complaints of inmates seen working on other farms, taking work from other local people."

"That's just ridiculous," James rumbled. "Idle talk and jealousy."

"So, you agree it happens?" Emmett said. The only reply was James's dark look. "My employer, Mr. Mitchener, would like me to investigate further. Inspect the books and so on. But…"

Emmett let the word hang in the air. The Turners exchanged a glance.

"But," he continued, "I want to be as flexible as I can. We need not have excess oversight. Truth is, we have a rash of new inmates coming and Mount Hope is full. The definition of insanity is being… refined. Plans are in place to add two new dormitories."

"More?" Eunice said, face pale. "We're over-full even now. We'll need more staff—"

"Nothing I can do there, I'm afraid. The tender is for new buildings only."

"Listen, you young upstart," James said, drawing near the pale Emmett. "You come here first accusing us, then telling us we have to work harder."

Emmett backed away, palms raised in fright. Eunice put a cautionary hand on her husband's shoulder.

"I understand," Emmett said. "I'm here to help with these changes. If you let me come and assist. For example, with that young man who was mute. What's his name?"

"You want to help with Stewart?" James said, anger replaced by surprise.

"Yes," Emmett said, relieved at James's change and at avoiding having to stammer the boy's name. "As you say, I

am young. I don't want to be always stuck with the Overseers. I want to change things for the better. Maybe I can
start by helping you at this farm."

He glanced around the shabby dining room. "Looks
like you could use some help. And," he paused again, to
stress the point. "no more going to the newspapers. Let
me do anything like that."

James sat down, chuckling softly to himself. Eunice
looked from one man to another, then forced a smile.

"This is fine news, Emmett," she said. "We're delighted
to have more official help. It's a lonely row we furrow out
here by the sea. Won't you come and see the rest of the
buildings? Where we do the sewing, the kitchen and
dormitories and so on. James has plenty to be doing out
on the farm, I'm sure."

Emmett allowed himself to be escorted around the
place. He hardly registered the wooden beds, the spartan
kitchen and other trivial details. His mind fixated on
Stewart and what he represented. He pictured putting
him in a gilded box and closing him up in there, kept for a
special future.

Application for admission

Application is herewith made to have here give name of person}...*Theresa O'Regan...* a pauper, from, and chargeable to District No. ...*18*... in the County of Halifax, admitted to the County Poors' Farm, to be maintained here in accordance with the rules and regulations of the institution, at the cost of said District No. ...*18*...
The said ...[Name of person.]...*Theresa O'Regan...* is ...*about 60*... years old.
native place—or nationality ...[if known.] ... *County of Halifax...*
Religion...............*Roman Catholic...*
is...[Say if sane—or sound]......*unsound mind...*
is...[Say if idiotic—or insane.].......*Idiotic Simple...*
......is...[Say if violent—or variable.]......*Mild...*
Condition...[Married or Single.].................*Single...*
Occupation or Trade...................*None...*
[State here if afflicted with any incurable, contagious or infectious diseases]......*Spastic. Botched forceps delivery...*

And we herewith agree for said District No. ... *18*... to pay quarterly through our Treasurer...[Give name and address.]...*John Stephen Mitchener...* to the Commissioners of said Poors' Farm the prescribed amount of

$...*1.00*... per week, for maintenance during the time said ...*Theresa O'Regan*...remains there.
Dated at ...*Waverley*...this...*12*...day of... *June*...1888

<table>
<tr><td>John Stephen</td><td rowspan="3">}</td><td>Overseers of Poor for District</td></tr>
<tr><td>A. R. Temple</td><td>No. ...18...</td></tr>
<tr><td>E. D. Forrestall</td><td>County of Halifax</td></tr>
</table>

Districts desiring to place persons on the Poors' Farm must, through their Overseers of Poor, make application on the prescribed form, and forward it to the County Clerk for examination and approval of the Commissioners of the Farm, and if they find everything in proper form and the party eligible, the order for admission will forthwith be granted.

Reverend

Poor Farm, Cole Harbour, 1890

"Thank you, Pastor, for coming to see us on a Wednesday," Eunice said, ushering the Reverend Cuthbert Powell up the narrow stairs of the Women's dormitory.

Powell was a full-figured man and panted a little at the exertion of scaling the stairs. "It is my deepest pleasure, Eunice," he said, cheeks flushed and slight perspiration on the pale downy hair of his upper lip. "As James says, '*Is anyone among you sick? Let him call for the elders of the church...*'"

Eunice smiled and nodded, expressing her comfort from this citation. But she could not help but notice the complacent tone to his plummy voice.

"Who have you for me today?" he asked.

"Down at the end, there's Tess. Theresa O'Regan. Everyone calls her Tess."

"Oh?"

"Yes. Probably Catholic, but she's hard to understand. We have a hard time getting a priest out here, even when they die."

Cuthbert tut-tutted at this, shaking his head at the indolence of his Papist co-religionists. "Perhaps a conversion might be possible," he murmured. Then, louder: "Do lead on!"

"Conversion?" Eunice said. "I should warn you, she can be difficult. She's been demanding a minister for a while and won't say why."

"The truth of Jesus will ease her troubles" Cuthbert said, enthusiastically heading down to the end room now that he had recovered from the toil of scaling the stairs. Eunice followed, a wary look on her face.

The little room had three wooden beds crammed in, covered by rough woollen ticking. A diminutive woman with a hunchback sat alone on one bed, a walking stick by her side. Like her twisted hands, her face contorted and her mouth often gaped open.

Her eyes, though, were bird-bright, studying the corpulent minister bumbling into the room. "Oo're not a priest. Fukin' Pastor! 'S no good.'

Cuthbert drew back in shock. "Did she... Did she just say what I think she said?"

"Tess," Eunice said, "behave now. The Reverend is here to tend to your spiritual needs."

"I need Conpession!" Tess announced. She pressed her lips together and stared out the window with annoyance. This took a while, as her control over her features was slow and unreliable.

"Good Heavens, what could she have to confess?" Cuthbert asked Eunice in an undertone. He turned to Tess, raising his voice.

"You don't need a sacrament for that, dear. Modern Christians simply confess together before God and then I can say a prayer of pardon."

"Can hear you fine," she snapped, slowly fixing her eye on him. "Want to conpess."

"Yes," Cuthbert pressed. "If you confess, I will see you are forgiven. Perhaps you will see then how much better we Methodists are as a religion."

Eunice sat on another of the beds, keeping a mistrustful eye on the older woman. She reflected on the time

Tess whacked one of the children with her stick; she wasn't so crippled when she wanted something.

"Dirty thoughts," she continued. "Fancy one...the men. Henry Harrow. One of...the Black fellas. Asked him...come bed me."

Cuthbert made a face.

"Well, that's...That's unfortunate. Mustn't associate with the inferior races, you know. That's why they bear the mark of Cain, their dark skin."

She considered this, rocking a little on the bed.

"Are you contrite?" Cuthbert said after the silence had extended beyond what he considered necessary. "Are you sorry for doing this? If you say yes, we can forgive you."

She paused for a long while. Cuthbert sweated beside her, waiting on her words.

Then Tess erupted into a fit of whooping laughter, eyes creased closed with mirth. "Am a hoor but won't be your hoor! Fukin' Protestants think you could catch me that easy."

She cackled with laughter as Cuthbert's face blanched with shock. He stood up quickly, brushing off his clothes as if she had soiled them.

"Tess," Eunice said, coming to his aid. "I'll see you're punished for this. Talking to clergy like that—"

"Shudup," Tess said. "Yer another hoor—"

Eunice sent a quick slap across the old woman's face. Her twisted hands went uselessly to shield herself from more blows, but she kept up her heaving laughter.

"Come, Pastor. Let's not give her any more satisfaction. She will be duly reprimanded for this behaviour. Have no fear. Won't you come down to our parlour for some tea and perhaps cake?"

"What terrible behaviour," he said, indignant. "Perhaps we should call in Father Sullivan to perform an exorcism."

The Washhouse

Poor Farm, Cole Harbour, Early Summer, 1890

Sally set down the large wicker basket and surveyed the pale grey blanket of fog all about her.

"*Fog on the hill brings water to the mill,*" she recited. "*Fog in the hollow means a fine day will follow.*"

She was on her way to the washhouse and still on high ground, near the main cluster of buildings. *Can't see them at all. Expect we'll have a wet day.*

She inhaled deeply, closing her eyes to enjoy the cool droplets on her face. It had been hot and close the last few days and the respite was welcome.

She licked her lips, the faintest tang of salt there. She opened her eyes. She pictured the sea stretching away eastwards, though she couldn't see it. The sheltered estuary was calm as a lake, but it was still the sea.

How long before moving on? She had escaped Cape Breton, the scandal and threats. If she saved up a little more, she might go further. It would have to be far this time, she reflected, to ensure anonymity. What was to keep her here?

She peered down into the basket full of soiled bed ticking, nose wrinkling at the pungent odour. Another sigh. She heaved it onto her hip and kept on the path towards the shore.

The washhouse was rickety, one of the old Roche farm buildings. The stove pipe disappeared into the foggy gloom. They fed the furnace all year round to heat the water.

Sally unlatched the door, pausing as her breath caught on the dense steamy atmosphere within. It always felt like crawling into a kettle.

She spied Hugh Morash on his knees: red-faced, feeding lumber into the grate. He gave her a vulpine grin, straightening up. "Come down to have a steamy time with me, Sally?"

She blinked in surprise at his newfound confidence. He had avoided her company since she hit at him, skulking away whenever she came near.

She put down the basket carefully and turned to face him. He was eyeing her with relish.

"We could have a nice hot time here," he said. There was a little caution in his voice despite this new bravado.

"Thought I smelled something foul in here." Sally rubbed her nose. "You're awful forward, all of a sudden. Don't you remember last time?"

He shrugged, making an indifferent face. "Met one of my buddies in Irishtown the other night. From up your part of the world. Baddeck, isn't it? He had some very interesting things to say about the McMahons up there."

It was Sally's turn to feign indifference. She said nothing but started feeding dirty clothing into one of the bubbling cauldrons.

"Heard quite a story: a child given up, the father a sailor back to sea. Hearing me now?"

In his excitement, Hugh drew near. Sally stopped what she was doing to stare hard at the wall.

"What a shame if the Turners heard about it." He was close now, taking her silence as an opportunity.

Sally turned and gave him a hard slap. "You say what you want about me," she said in a low voice. "I'll tell them how you attacked me when I was alone. I'll even run out of here with my shirt loose. Let's see who they believe."

He held a hand to his crimson cheek in disbelief. In her fury at being discovered, she had hit him hard.

"You need to be taught a lesson," he said. "You'll be thrown out of here like before."

"Maybe. I don't think you have the goods, though."

He went for her then. She was ready and pushed the large vat of angry water into his way. He squealed in pain at the shock of scalding, and folded over. The fetid smell of the resident's night-soiled "doidies" fouled the air.

"What is going on here!" Eunice asked, peering into the steam from the doorway.

Sally was first to recover. "Are you alright, Mr. Morash? Matron, he was helping me with the laundry and the tub slipped."

Hugh glared at Sally, lips set in pain. A look of understanding passed between them. A truce.

"It's nothing. I'll...I'll be fine."

"Dear me." Eunice bustled in. "What a mess!"

Several minutes of confusion followed as the pair tried to right the tub in the narrow space under Eunice's instructions. Hugh spoke little and left as soon as he could, shirt and pants soaking.

Eunice gave a skeptical side-glance to Sally as they watched him depart. "What really happened here?" Her tone was even, without accusation.

Sally turned away, bending down to pick up laundry, filthy now from the dirt floor.

"Miss McMahon." Eunice was stern now. "If anything untoward happened, I want you to alert me immediately."

Sally plopped most of the garments onto the mat. Her face was flushed and her breathing quick. It wasn't from the exertion. *Surprising*, she thought, *how he got to me like that*. She decided on honesty. "I can handle a nuisance like Hugh Morash, Matron."

Eunice drew her head back, shocked. There was risk here, for both of them. Then she gave a tight nod. "You watch these men. They'll try anything. Especially that one."

Sally shrugged. "He's a bantam cock. All noise, but nothing behind it."

A giggle burst through Eunice's strict demeanour. Sally marvelled at the complete change to the Matron's face.

"The way he dolls himself up on the weekend," Eunice chortled. "Puffed up in that tatty little waistcoat."

They both laughed hard, more than expected, sudden tears of mirth in the sweaty space. Deep relief in Sally at not having to be so careful.

Eunice eased herself down onto a small stool. "Say nothing to James, mind." Eunice wiped her eyes. "He might not say much, but he can get worked up about... these things. A real stickler for the church."

Sally nodded, sitting down on an upturned basket.

"Speaking of church." Eunice's small smile was conspiratorial. "We had Pastor Powell on Wednesday."

"I saw him leave in an awful hurry."

"He met his match in old Tess. Oh, she can be a dragon." Eunice shook her head. "Had to give her a slap. Not that she minded. What she said to the reverend..."

"You know she's—"

"One of your lot? Yes. The good pastor was eager for a conversion and she relished the opportunity to lash out. By the finish, he was looking to Rome for your best exorcist."

Sally grinned. It seemed to be the day for truces. *Must be the change in the weather.*

"Sally?" A change to Eunice's voice, almost querulous. "I want you to do more with Stewart. This Mr. Forrestall has taken an interest and I need your help. I'll get Alice to do more of the washing and mending so you can...lend a hand."

"'Course, Matron. I love helping with Stewart."

"It was you found his voice that first time. Far as I can tell, he likes your company."

"Thank you. I'm fond of him, too." Sally looked down, thinking of how she had been planning on quitting the farm.

"Make sure you sing to him. That's a lovely voice you have. And we need to keep this Mr. Forestall entertained. We have had...questions about the operation of the farm and he—"

"I understand, Matron." Sally had heard the rumours.

"Not a bad-looking fellow, I suppose." Sally was double-shocked by Eunice's implication and salacious cackle. "You could do worse..."

"Matron! Never thought I'd hear such talk from you."

"I may be as old as this creaking washhouse, but I was young, too."

She hauled herself off the little stool. "Don't be worrying about Hugh Morash, either. I got cornered by the likes of him a long time ago. Wish I'd scalded him..."

Sally's eyes widened at the revelation. "Matron. That's terrible. I—"

Eunice shook it off, her lined face settling back to its usual mask. "Not to worry. Ancient history. Just know I'll protect you. Come now. Let's get that wash out and tend the stove. It will be coming onto lunch soon and we should get back up."

~

Fog, turning to drizzle, licked at the windows of the men's building. Sally stumbled a bit as she entered. The connecting corridor to the Centre Wing was an afterthought addition with an unexpected half-step.

Andrew MacDonald was supervising a group in the common room. They were attempting to weave baskets from raffia. It was Matron's idea. Jean Paul, a burly Mi'kmaq man, had cast his attempt to the ground and was batting at his face, caught in a hopeless cycle of frustration.

"Sally," Andrew called, "can you help me out here? I think Mr. Paul needs some quiet time."

"Can't." Sally said, breezing by them. "I'm to only help with Stewart. Matron's orders."

Andrew's brows furrowed at her tart tone. "I'm sure she'd want you to help calm him." Annoyance was plain in Andrew's voice. "Get Jenny, then."

Sally shrugged and headed back to the women's building. As a young woman, Jenny had been taken from her impoverished family some years back and was now almost one of the staff. Lately, she had taken to calling a few of the men her boyfriends.

When Sally returned with Jenny in tow, Jean had escalated to yelling at Andrew.

"There's my favourite boyfriend. What's wrong with you, you crazy Indian?" Always nervous, Jenny rapid-fire spoke in short brittle sentences. "Jean! Stop yelling so. You'll upset Andrew. We all know he's the best one here."

Jenny folded her skinny arms around the big man. His big shoulders relaxed as she talked him into a nearby chair.

Andrew shook his head, watching the pair warily. There had been births between inmates and he worried there might be more.

Sally took advantage of the distraction to slip upstairs. She found Stewart sitting on a bed. He stared right through her as she stood in the doorway.

"Good day, Mr. Stewart," she said brightly. "I think we'll be spending a lot more time together."

There was no response. He did not even blink.

"Away with the fairies, are you?"

Her grandmother's expression gave her an idea, her variation on a nursery rhyme. "How about this one?"

Sally plopped down on the bed beside him. She ignored the scurry of insects at the side of the straw-filled mattress.

> The king was in his counting house,
> Counting out his money...

She held his hand, pretending to count out money. Still no response. His hand limp. Sally changed from reciting to half-singing the rhyme.

> The queen was in the parlour,
> Eating bread and honey.

Elaborate miming of a queen. She stage-whispered, "Like Eunice."

Slightest blink from Stewart.

"The maid," she indicated herself, "was in the garden..."

> Hanging out the clothes,
> When down came a blackbird,

Sally's hand hovered in the air.

> And *pinched* off her nose.

She made a grab for his nose.

He didn't like it at first, wiping furiously. Neither would he look at her hand for the removed nose, as most children might.

Sally put her hands down, singing the last addition from her grandmother:

> And she swore by the cross,
> She'd never go to Mass.
> Then she played Pitch and Toss,
> On the Blackbird's ass.

Stewart's eyes opened wide at the new verse. She took advantage of his interest by tickling him. He beamed broad with excitement.

"Again."

She repeated the rude last verse several times, to much raucous laughter.

Beginning to tire, Sally feared someone might hear and take offence. "Come on," she whispered. "How about we play something else? Do you know 'Hide and Go Seek'?"

His features shut down once more.

"Again," he repeated, sullen.

"Come *on*, Stewart. Don't you know how to play? You go hide somewhere and I'll try and find you."

He considered for a while before standing up.

"Play Pitch a' Toss on Blackbird's Ass." His grin was all mischief.

Sally gave a wary "All right" before he tore out of the room, shouting the rude ending all the while.

"Oh, you little bugger!"

She raced after him, following the trail of his laughter. Clattering down the narrow stairs, she looked around the common room.

"Hey," Andrew called, "I'm sure you're not allowed have him run around like that."

"He's not allowed to run wild," Jenny interjected "Disrupts the rest of us."

"That's right," Jean Paul said. "That lad's a right arse."

Sally ignored them, running to the laughter she could hear from the hall to the Centre Wing. She just heard "Blackbird's Ass" as she turned the corner, spotting Stewart wriggling in James's arms.

"Keeper!"

James had his hand clamped over Stewart's mouth. He stared hard at Sally.

"I would have him outside," Sally apologized. "Only it's raining out now."

"Why are you—? Ow!" He sharply withdrew his hand, wringing it from Stewart's bite.

"Matron told me to mind Stewart more. I'll take him somewhere else. Keep him quieter. Come here, Stewart."

Sally disentangled the youth from James. He held his big hand, scrutinizing the mark near a calloused knuckle.

"This is not a...nursery!" he erupted.

The surprising shout echoed in the small hallway. Sally's eyes went wide as she and Stewart froze. James's face was a crimson blush of rage.

"You are a servant, Miss McMahon. Behave like one."

Sally bit her lower lip and nodded.

"I'll...I will speak with the Matron about your duties. Return this...inmate to the others."

He stormed off toward the kitchen.

Sally swallowed with worry, only then noticing Stewart's hand in hers.

~

You always want the songs over and over again. There is a moment, in a song, where it is perfect. Like that time at the sea when you stuck your head into a wave. You saw all along its curve. The water turned to glass and paused, for once still. An eternity later, the whole lot crashed, and you were coughing up salt-water.

But that's what you love: to stand outside the world and look on it, not to be caught up with it. Like that song with the magician, if you could only hold time still and perfect.

Even right now, before the Keeper caught you: your laughing was music you could see in the air all around. Running just ahead of the turn of time. The dull misery of the farm like the lead sea and you a wave above and within it. You come from it, but you are also out of it.

Sally, always on the shoreline, calling for you.

Then you turned and crashed into the Keeper. He was hard as black rocks. You flailed and thrashed to stay afloat. To go back to that single pristine moment. But the music faded like an echo and you cried and called for it back.

No. It was only back to the farm and the knifing eye of the Keeper. So you bit him and he let go. When you ran free in the woods, was it a dog that bit you in the dark?

You think of the ghost you often see around the farm. She is about your age. Like you: she does not speak. No one else sees her.

You envy how she is stuck in a moment forever, but pity her, too. Especially to be stuck in *this* place. She walks down the corridor, past everyone else's vision. *Why don't they see her?* She lost someone and is always, always seeking them.

The others keep eating, laughing, nodding together as she trudges by, unseen and silent. Sometimes they close a cupboard she had opened. They might even pause and wonder how it had come loose. Then they would shrug and keep on. Never stopping to see her *right there.*

Once. Maybe she saw you? Her black sad eyes looked in your direction. Recognizing you. An offer to join her.

You froze, a hare caught in the lamplight. Would it be so terrible to join her?

But fear caught you and you ripped at everything all about, screaming. Escape her icy touch at all costs.

No one understood. They had to tie you down.

You watch in terror as she stumbles about the room, looking for something. Always looking. This time it is you.

Madder than a wet hen

Poor Farm, Cole Harbour, Early Summer, 1890

They had painted the walls of the hen house with creosote to keep the fetid odour of droppings out of the timber. The result was a gloomy cave of hens roosting on white-splattered shelves, clucking warily at each other.

Eunice had a chicken by the claws and was dipping its head into a bucket of cold water. The fowl shook all over and attempted to peck her, eyes vicious with indignation.

James burst through the door, his jaw outthrust—a prow leading his furious body forward. "What're you doing?" he barked.

She took a step back, releasing the bird. "What's it look like? A few of the hens are broody. I'm wetting them to calm them down. Keeps them laying. What's got into *you*?"

He wild-cast his gaze around the room, looking for spies amongst the hens.

"That Sally McMahon." His breath was heaving. "She's running around the men's building after Stewart. That hellion bit me."

"Did you try and stop him?" Eunice stood arms akimbo, lips pursed.

"Of course. He was out of control."

"What if you had let him go?"

"We're not running a *nursery*, Eunice. He has to learn... Did you? Did you tell Sally to run around after him?"

"I told her to play with him, yes."

"That's ridiculous," he said. "We can't run things like that."

"Like *what*?" Eunice's blink was as calm as a cat's.

"For the whim of every inmate, is what. Next you'll have Jenny taking one of her beaus to a dance or...or Ned Beales to the Academy of Music."

Eunice knew to wait out his rage. Normally taciturn, every so often James's simmering pot boiled over. It never lasted. "Would all that be so bad?"

He made a disgusted sound. "Eunice. I'm trying to run this place properly." The exasperation in his voice sounded like the worst was over.

"James. We talked about this. We work flat out to keep this place together and nobody cares. Worse. For whatever reason, they're after us now. Asking questions. We need a distraction. You saw how Forrestall was taken by Stewart. What harm if Sally runs around with him for a while during the day? A little success story will do us good."

"And Sally?" he growled. "Getting notions above her station?"

Eunice's shrug was slight and weary. "I don't know. She seems a good girl..."

With a scornful look, James turned to leave. Eunice reached out and caught his arm.

"I'll talk to her," she promised. "No more running around inside. Let them head out around the woods once in a while. It'll help us. You'll see."

He took a few deep breaths, not looking at his wife. Then he nodded, and strode out the door. Eunice was left alone, the hens warbling their opprobrium.

~

"Go and tell Aunt Nabbie," Sally's voice rang above the hush of the waves.

"Go a' tell Aun' Nabbie," Stewart answered, a quirk of a smile on his face.

"Go and tell Aunt Nabbie." She patted his shoulder. *Would he get the last line?*

"The old grey goose is dead."

She ha-hahed aloud. He shot her a pleased look.

They cleared the woods, coming on the dirt road by the shore.

"The one she was a-saving for,"

She waited. No response. He gazed blithely down to the water.

"The one she was a-saving for,"

Still nothing. She tutted her disappointment.

"The one she was a-saving for,"

"To make a feather bed."

She finished the verse, wondering how to make him join in again.

"The last verse's simple. You know it:"

> *He died easy,*
> *He died easy,*
> *He died easy,*
> *A-standing on his head.*

He walked ahead. She didn't see the smirk on his face. Then she heard him mumbling the first line again: "Go a' tell Aunt Nabbie".

"Oh, that's your game, is it?" Sally ran up to him and tickled him. "You only want to sing the first verse."

The sun peered down on them through a circle of heavy clouds. They picked their way along the dunes, smelling of ozone from the previous day's rain. The sea grass was rampant with purple orchids and wild roses.

"Who needs a fancy garden when you can wander out here?" she murmured.

Stewart—always walking a few steps behind her—did not reply. He was busy making repetitive motions with his fingers.

"What does it mean when you do that?" she said. "Is it one of those signs they say Helen Keller makes for Miss Sullivan? Oh, what a story if we could make you speak properly too, Stewart. I could be your special nurse. I don't think Emmett Forrestall is anywhere near as smart as Mr. Bell, though. Now, there's a true gentleman. I saw in *The Chronicle* how he does all manner of wonderful experiments up in Cape Breton. Imagine."

She peered at their first glimpse of the sea beyond the dunes. "We have a break from the farm today, anyway. I think we went a bit too far yesterday: upset the Keeper. Better to be out of there, for once. A bit of a picnic and then a swim. What do you think of that, Stewart?"

Stewart, unable to contain himself any longer, ran past to the broad beach. The giddy sing-song noise he made had a happy ring to it. Sally shook her head and moved the basket from one hand to the other.

"Oh!" she exclaimed when she reached the beach. Stewart's clothes and shoes were in a pile at the edge of the dune grass. A set of pigeon-toed footprints led down to where she could see his shockingly pale bare bottom.

Sally giggled, putting the basket down next to the clothes. *He loves to swim naked.* She laid out a blanket and pitched down on it. Shading her eyes, she watched him thrash about, smiling and slapping at the water. *Good thing no one ever comes down here.*

"Be careful!" she called. "There might be a current."

Her words might as well have been the plovers' piping at the water's edge: he paid so little notice.

It got dull again, low clouds drifting in from the far shore of the swift river that emptied from the estuary into the sea. Sally fished in the basket for an apple. She chose the smaller of the two and bit a sizable chunk from it. Munching, she scanned the deserted beach. There were only cormorants about, some on the rocks spreading their black wings. One flew across the shoreline, opening and closing its mouth but making no sound.

Sally lay back and closed her eyes. Dozing, she thought about the real Stewart, the child she had given up for adoption. She thought of him every day. She had vowed on the first day to do so. It helped make the hurt less. Often she would picture what he might be like today. In her daydream, she pictured him as a tall teenager, talking excitedly to her.

~

"That child." Her mother's tone was final. "Has to go."

"You listen to your mother. 'Fore you get too attached."

Her father was soot black. Back up from the mine. His eyes were unnaturally white, glaring at her. Their little house had a permanent sheen of black. She and her sisters chored regularly to keep it at bay.

"It's your own fault," her mother said. "I warned you about that sailor."

Sally ignored the malicious relish in her mother's voice. She thought of Michael and his roguish smile. She had known whatever he was promising wasn't true, but at least it was kind. At the dance, he had twirled her about as they laughed. She only saw him a few times.

Enough for her mother to get wind of it through their small community.

She pictured the mine as a lake of blackness under their feet, darkening everyone's hearts. *What if she kept him? What life would he have?* Maybe a wealthy family like the Bells would take her baby and raise him properly. Better than she could, both of them shunned and a spectacle for the hard-scrabble mining community.

The next day her father, scrubbed clean and shaven, brought the nun in. He would be well taken care of, the sister insisted. Her hairy chin peered out from under a black habit.

Sally held onto the child one last time. She stared at his dimpled cheeks and the little fuzz on his head. Like her own: his eyes were pale grey, not blue. His little arms were plump. All of him shone in her arms, a bundle of light. He didn't cry either, so she held her own tears. *Time for that later.*

"That's all done now." Father declared, closing the door. A black gap within her sucked her breath away, like holding a newspaper in front of the fireplace to make the fire draw. She thought she could faint and perhaps wake up with the baby next to her.

Her mother wiped a plate, nonchalantly humming. *That did it.*

She leaped at her mother, screaming. She belted her in the eye properly, the way her brother had taught her. She wondered at the triumphant sneer on her mother's face even as the blow landed. She lashed and tore some more at the old dragon until her father hit her hard on the back of the head. Her vision filled with a flash of ochre yellow before the kitchen went black.

~

Sally jerked awake with a start. There was no sign of her charge. Grabbing a swath of calico that they used as a towel, she ran down toward the water. The tide had gone out.

"Stewart! Where are you, Stewart?"

Her voice had a frantic edge to it. Everyone at the farm knew Stewart could swim—Andrew had had to fish him out of the deep well twice already.

"Stewart! Oh, Stewart," she called to the mild waves, starting to sob now. The water was up to her knees and frigid. Her feet were so numb from the cold, she marvelled at how he had even got into it.

Looking out at the dark blue of the ocean, she inhaled deeply and squared her shoulders. He had done this before. *Why was she surprised this time?* There was no sign of anything to her right. She could see the distant rise of the promontory at the end of the bay. She turned to her left, where the estuary emptied into the sea.

She ran.

The beach turned inland and spread out to a broad, flat expanse. She spotted him stretched at the edge where the swift water of the river met with the receding tide. His thin white body reminded her of an unnatural white fish writhing at the bottom of a bucket.

"Stewart! Stewart! Are you all right?"

Sally pounded across the sand, her feet sometimes slipping on the greasy dark ground.

She stopped.

He was intensely twiddling a piece of seaweed, lying there smiling at it.

She heaved a heavy sigh and trudged slowly up to him.

"Cover yourself, Stewart," she commanded, giving him the large cloth. "Oh, you gave me some fright. I thought you had been swept out to sea!"

She erupted into tears, crumpling helplessly down on the damp sand.

Stewart sat up, hugging the fabric around his bony shoulders. He was smiling. "Abenture," he said.

~

"You and your adventure," Sally said as she led him back to the picnic basket. "Nearly gave me a heart attack, Stewart. Here, get your trousers on."

He struggled with the garment.

"No, no. You've it backwards. Here, show me."

It took a while to get it straightened out. Sally flopped down onto the rug. "That is enough excitement for me, thank you. Imagine what the Keeper would have done to me if I'd let you drown? He'd have me out on the street, no doubt about it."

He was lying on his belly in the sand, staring at the granules sifting through his fingers.

"But you said *Adventure*. Well done! First time I've heard you say that. And it was an adventure, too."

She considered him. "Imagine if you could talk more? Then we really could go on an adventure. Escape the Farm and make our own way. I'd look after you, Stewart. I know your ways. What you like and...don't like. Where could we go?"

She took a deep breath, folding her arms as her mind examined possibilities. "Why stop at Halifax? Why not go to Montreal or Boston? I'll find us—"

He stood up and started stamping the sand, wringing his hands in agitation. "No! No-no-no. No go."

She stood and went to him, wide-eyed. He had never insisted on something with this clarity. She gently stroked his back. "It's alright, Stewart," she soothed. "No. We won't go anywhere, if you don't want to go. Here, sit down here on the rug and have some cheese."

He slowly sat beside her, snatching the cheddar she had retrieved from the basket. She frowned as he mangled the cheese between his fingers, over and over. "Do try and eat it, Stewart."

She cleared a strand of unruly hair from his forehead. "I wonder why you're so anxious to stay."

There was no reply from Stewart. He munched on the cheese, agitation from a few moments ago forgotten.

Sally lay back on the rug. "I suppose we can wait a bit until we have a better plan," she murmured.

She watched him regurgitate the cheese, play with it a little, then swallow it again. Over and over.

Mother

George Street, Halifax, 1890

"Mr. Forrestall. You have a visitor. It's about an inmate of the poor farm," Arthur said to Emmett, who was sidling in from a late lunch.

"Who is it?" he hissed, looking over to the cloud of pipe smoke in the corner. Mitchener was in the office for once.

"Wouldn't say unless she was speaking to an Assessor." Arthur was all diffident innocence. "She said it was important. I put her in the interview room."

They had a small side room for interviews. Family members being signed away often required privacy. Emmett regarded Arthur with suspicion. *Why hadn't Mitchener interviewed her?*

"Her? All right. I'll be there directly."

He dropped his jacket at his desk. His superior made no remark, staring out the window while puffing on his pipe. He reminded Emmett of a distant mountain shrouded in mist. He considered asking for clarification, but thought better of it. Perhaps the old man hadn't noticed his late arrival.

The interview room had a clammy feel to it; mildew crept up the walls. A middle-aged woman in a tattered dress sat in a plain chair. Cheap powder and rouge covered a weather-beaten face, eyebrows inexpertly blackened and thin lips garishly reddened.

"Ah, hello. Madam." Emmett wasn't absolutely sure she was female. "My name is Emmett Forrestall. I'm an Assessor here. You wished to speak about the poor farm."

"Yes. Indeed I do." Her harsh voice was accented. *West of Ireland?* Emmett guessed. "That's my son ye have out there on that poor farm."

"Your son? Just a moment. And what might your name be?" He almost slipped into their cadence of speech, although he hadn't lived there long enough to pick it up.

"Me? I'm Florence Mulvaney. My son's name is Seamus. Lost him a number of years back. He ran off, so he did. I didn't know the county had taken him."

"Didn't know?" Emmett raised a skeptical eyebrow. "Please bear with me while I check the register of inmates."

"Ye probably don't have the right name on him. Seeing as how he was never found proper. He's the one that's been in the paper. Mute he was as a child, too. But he loved to sing."

"The mute boy?" Emmett almost let the name slip out. The thought of stammering it saved him. "Do you know his name?" He was half-standing, about to leave to get the ledger.

"Don't care what name ye've put on him. Seamus is his proper name. Seamus Mulvaney. A right handful he was as a babe. 'Course his father took off for the Boston states. No more work on the canal and his belly full of drink. Never heard from him again either. Seamus kept running off, and I had me hands full with the older ones."

Emmett plopped back down in his chair. "Why did you wait? All this time."

"Didn't know what to do, did I? Was in the Bridewell myself for a spell. But I'm out now and I want what's mine. 'Specially now I hear he's got a talent."

"Talent?" All Emmett could do was dumbly repeat what she said.

"Might get him into the circus. Or one of them shows? Friend of mine...Well, never mind. I've got connections. See, I've not been well of late and could do with some money."

"There are laws against putting children to work."

"That's what ye do out there, isn't it? Putting my poor Seamus to work night and day for all them rich farmers along the shore. Only because he can't speak. Out there with those Blacks and Indians. But he has the voice of an angel. My angel."

She affected to hide her eyes, as if overcome. Astonished as he was, Emmett was skeptical of this display of emotion.

"Wait there, Mrs. Mulvaney. I have to consult my superior."

She sobbed theatrically, her face buried in her hands, but Emmett noticed she cocked an ear at this information. He closed the door and hurried to Mitchener's desk.

"Mister Forrestall?" the older man said sedately. For once, he had his pipe put aside and Emmett had an unobstructed view of his leonine features.

"There's a woman come to claim St-st-st...A child in the poor farm, as hers."

"A child?"

"He may be as old as fourteen. We're not sure."

"You know the person?"

"I do. He's...an interesting case. He sings. Although we thought him entirely mute."

Mitchener's mouth opened. Whatever he was to say halted as he considered this. "You go out there to hear a mute sing?"

Emmett laughed nervously at the suspicious rumble in his boss's voice. "Not that *per se*. You see, I was attempting to encourage his rehabilitation. He truly is a remarkable case. It could make an exemplary case for the Overseers, if I...were we to have a celebrated discovery of a treatment for mutism."

Mitchener's prominent brow furrowed. "May I remind you, Mr. Forrestall, that our primary purpose is to keep the tax-paying citizens of this County safe from those who will not work. There is a certain cost to this. If this woman is the young fellow's parent, then we should return him to her. Or they will *celebrate* us entirely differently than you imagine."

"Cost?" Emmett asked, his voice hopeful. "That should deter her. She will have to cover the cost of his detention for however many years."

"Hmm. there is that," Mitchener said. "Typically, we don't pursue that too strenuously—"

"And she has a record. She said she did a spell in the Bridewell. You could put a word in with Marshall Cotter, find out her background?"

Mitchener stared hard at his underling. His next words were full of affront. "I am not in the habit of calling on the head of the city police on a whim. I will leave this matter for you to resolve properly. Mr. Forrestall."

Emmett nodded a few times, his mind occupied with various schemes. He returned to the little interview room after rifling through his desk for a form.

"Ah, Madam. I have here a claim form for you to complete. An official st-st-statement. It requires certain details, such as," he read off the document. "*Description of distinguishing marks on the body.*"

She glared at him, snapping the page from his hand and squinting at it. It was the wrong form, but Emmett was positive she couldn't read.

"I'm not signing anything! I just want what's rightfully mine. Are you telling me you won't give him back?"

"There are procedures to follow. We need to establish that you are capable of caring for the child. You said yourself you had issues with the law. And there is the matter of payment…"

"Payment! What the Jaysus do you mean? I'm going to look after him, amn't I?"

Emmett noted her righteous anger was a lot more authentic than her grief.

"The County has been looking to his care for several years. That cost must be recouped. If you are his rightful guardian."

As with Mitchener, Emmett found a mouth agape before him. Hers was a horrid pit of blackened stumps. She stood up, quivering with rage.

"You jacked-up stuttering Jinnet! I'll give you 'recouped'. I want my son back! I'll…I'll go to my MP. Keep your hands off me!"

He stood back with a fixed smile, eyes on the wall. "Please, madam. I am only attempting to help. To do the best for the child."

She gathered her shawl about her and huffed out of the room. At the main door, she called back: "Overseers of the Poor, me arse! I know what ye're doing out there. Experiments on him, that's what it is. I heard all about it. I'll tell! There'll be papers who want to hear what kind of things are going on out there."

Mitchener reached for his pipe, outwardly ignoring the outburst. Emmett cocked his head to one side. *How did she know about the therapy?*

Arthur licked his lips and quietly closed the office door behind her.

Telephone

Poor Farm, Cole Harbour, May 1891

"Sit down there."

Stewart stood at the door to the Keeper's office. He twisted a piece of paper in his hands. Twisting it over and over.

Emmett regarded him for a long while. As Assessor for the Council, Emmett could use the little room for whatever he might need, although Turner always ushered him in with gruff suspicion. Emmett rubbed his eyes and sighed with exasperation. They had had several fruitless meetings. *It was time to try something new.*

He knew he should say the boy's name. He refused to try whatever name that dragon Mrs. Mulvaney had concocted. It sounded fine in his own head: 'Stewart'. But the sounds 'ST' and 'V' were the two demons prodding him with pitchforks throughout his circle of hell. No 'V' in 'Stewart', but 'W' was close enough to worry about.

He remembered the schoolmaster who taunted him to read some passage in front of the class. The burning of his cheeks. Standing there as they snickered and rolled their eyes. The teacher's tongue massaging his inner cheek as he struggled to hide a smile. *What would the Reverend Daddy Forrestall think?* he had chided.

"You understand me. I know that. It's v-v-very frustrating you don't follow my direction."

Stewart kept turning and twiddling the piece of paper, little flecks of it drifting to the floor. Emmett considered losing his patience. They had tried violence already, but with little tangible results.

After another sigh, he got up from behind the desk. "Come. Over here."

As Emmett held the chair, he produced a brown paper bag of humbugs from his pocket. He held one out.

Stewart darted forward, grabbing for the candy.

"Oh no. Sit down first."

With a scowl to the floorboards, Stewart sat. Emmett handed him the humbug. He straightaway started grinding it between his teeth, not stopping to suck at all.

"You'll have no teeth left, you keep that up," Emmett said. He accepted now it was better to coax the boy into performing an act. Violent coercion was ineffective. The child had remarkable powers of resistance. Emmett returned to his seat and made a note of this in his notebook.

"I am going to try a new treatment. I want you to look at this." Emmett produced a pendant, dangling it in front of the boy's eyes. A cheap bauble he had picked up at Cheapside market.

"Look at this. See how the light shines in it. I want you to relax, now. As the light spins, you feel relaxed and sleepy."

Emmett made up the prompts as he went. He deliberately kept them simple. The mesmerist he had seen at the Academy of Music had been long-winded, using ridiculous words that Stewart could not possibly understand. He had read a little about the topic and its effects. It seemed to be most effective on the weak-minded, a category his subject certainly fitted.

"I want you to feel relaxed and very sleepy. Watch the light in the crystal go back and forth."

Emmett spoke slowly and quietly. This practice loosened his tongue. Did he just say "very" without difficulty? It felt like he was doing this right.

Stewart frowned. He was actually looking at the pendant. *Could this be working?*

"That's good, Stewart. Stare into the depths of the crystal and relax. Only hear my voice and what I suggest to you."

Would he understand that? His subject was such a paragon. Perhaps this was a way to unlock the mystery.

Stewart stood up and walked to the window, looking directly at the mid-afternoon sun still refracting in Emmett's cheap pendant.

"Damn it! Why can you never sit st-st-still?" Emmett growled, his words catching on themselves. His mind too had wandered, imagining hypnotizing Stewart before a select audience of academics and philanthropists. The inheld breath of the crowd as Stewart's eyes flickered shut. Could Emmett drug him to reproduce this dramatic effect?

He snapped the swinging pendant into his palm with a single motion. Stewart made no response, absorbed in the scene outside the window.

~

A knock at the door.

"Yes. Come in," Emmett barked.

"Sorry, I don't mean to disturb you. Matron said to see if you wanted anything."

He blinked at Sally. An inky blob spread from where his fountain pen pressed too hard on his notebook.

"I. I was..." he faltered. "Um, come in."

She slipped into the small office, looking over at Stewart by the window. He had put the scrap of paper in his mouth and was chewing on it.

"Hullo, Stewart," she said. "How're you doing?"

"You? You speak to him?" Emmett asked, curiosity overcoming his usual tongue-tied manner around the girl.

"Sure," said Sally, dark red eyebrows raised in surprise. "Anyone can speak to Stewart."

"And he responds?"

She cocked her head to one side, considering the question. "In his own way. Don't you, Stewart?"

Stewart kept on staring out at the open field, the cumulus clouds scudding by and the sunlight shifting on and off.

"He won't say anything for me," Emmett said. "I'm wondering if this isn't a waste of my time."

"Maybe you're going about it wrong." Her tone was tart. "He likes it when I take him for walks. We talk most when we're allowed to go out together. Matron says you are studying him. Ever since..."

Emmett looked at her. She blushed a little under the scrutiny. "I mean. Ever since people got interested in his story."

"What kinds of things do you speak about?" he asked. He noted her unruly red hair had streaks of fair in it.

"Oh. The kinds of things you might say at a graveyard, I suppose. You know, to a dead relative." She, too, was gazing out the window now.

Emmett took the opportunity to stare at her. *What an extraordinary pale blue her eyes are.*

"You know they are there, but they can't answer back directly." Sally frowned then, coming to herself. "Sorry. I sometimes let my thoughts run away. What's that for?"

Emmett made a guilty grab for the pendant, his previous astonishment at the girl curdling to defensiveness.

"Just an experiment," he said. "I expect you wouldn't understand. We Overseers must try unusual methods for...for rehabilitation of the inmates."

"Like Anne Sullivan and Helen Keller?"

"Yes. I suppose so."

"I've been reading about her. In the paper. Anne Sullivan helped that poor girl speak and read and write. I told Stewart all about them."

"It's quite the story," Emmett agreed, ignoring the ridiculous idea of Stewart understanding any of this. *This girl has come unhinged, working out here.*

"My uncle Michael. He's up there in Baddeck. He's working on the Bell estate. They're building a huge house up there. Michael said Mr. Bell introduced Anne to Helen."

Emmett gaped at her. "You know Doctor Bell?"

"My uncle does. A bit. Anyway, I don't see Michael too much these days. Working down here."

"I'm sure a great genius like that hasn't much time for..." He stopped himself from saying "chatting with labourers" and gave her a guilty look.

Sally didn't notice. She was regarding Stewart with a keen eye. "Would he be interested, do you think? In Stewart?"

"Who? *Alexander Graham Bell?*"

Emmett can't stop himself from bursting out laughing. "The man who invented the telephone?" he asked, between bouts of mirth. "Interested in this little pimple of the world?"

Emmett surprised himself at how much he sounded like Mitchener just then. He took in her suddenly bashful features. She blushed easily.

"I suppose you could telephone him right now?" His humour curdled to mockery. "Have him come down?"

"No," she said, looking down. "Mr. Turner made it clear the women weren't to use the telephone. It is only to be used for important business."

"Yes," he said, recovering. "That is why Council approved the installation. Emergencies only."

"Well then," she said, and turned to the door. Over her shoulder, she added, "If you don't need anything else, I'll get back to my work."

Emmett watched her go, considering the strangeness of their conversation. "Quite an interesting friend you have there, St-St-Stewart." he said at last. He glanced over at the boy and jumped. Stewart was staring intently back at him.

Emmett's eyes widened, and he beamed at the boy as an idea took him. *Genius!* he proclaimed to himself.

"That's what I'll do. I'll get you to meet Alexander Graham Bell. It will change everything."

Field notes

The Poor Farm under my direction has found a child. Approximately ten to fourteen years of age. We cannot be sure. A farmer brought him to the farm's attention. Caught him trying to steal potatoes. Eating them raw from the drill in the field. He was wearing rags. We suspect his true parents abandoned him. The farmer thought him a wild beast at first. Later, he thought him incapable of speech. It was not clear if he was deaf or not.

Farmer and wife were astonished, afraid of him. Thought he might be half demon or wolf. How did he survive out there?

~

I have observed he is remarkably fastidious in his eating habits. For example, he will not touch fruit, no matter how hungry. This is intriguing, for he must have come across wild berries and fruit when living rough. Did he avoid them despite being near starvation? I have shut him in a room for a day now and left a plate of apples from the Valley. The wretch never even touched them. How to explain such a peculiar aversion?

~

He appears remarkably tolerant of pain. Were my eyes not opened to the world of science, I might fancy him possessed of the devil. Particularly when I tried several covert experiments testing his tolerance. Exposure to cold or repeated pricking with a pin do not seem to elicit any response that we would call normal. This may explain how he survived his time in the woods, especially as he was no doubt near starvation. How to explain this side of his nature, though? Empathy or even awareness of others seems utterly beyond him. It is not that he is mute, as was first thought, but that his soul is mute. Unresponsive and utterly cold.

~

Initially, the Keeper thought to bed him with the other inmates. However, I am told he wakes at all hours screaming with terror or laughter. This caused something of a rebellion against him, so they deemed it prudent to put him in a single room, until a better solution is forthcoming. They usually reserve this kind of treatment for the infirm, so initially they tried bedding him in the pantry. I am told by the Matron (who opposed this course of action) they awoke the next morning to the sounds of one of the help yelling that a ghost was in the kitchen. They rushed downstairs in their pyjamas to find the boy naked and covered in flour. He had been luxuriating in it all night long. What kind of creature is he, to find pleasure in such an act?

~

Continuation of experiments with extreme cold: I endeavoured to immerse the boy in a tub of cold sea water. Initially, he showed no objection to the frigid water. In fact, he seemed to delight in its effects and squealed and splashed excessively. Unfortunately, Matron interfered with my efforts, objecting to what she termed "cruel treatment of one of her care." I tried to explain my rationale, but she ignored me. They give any of my attempts at improvement of the mean circumstances of this institution the same reception.

~

Once, for variation, I took him to town in a buggy. I noticed a peculiar habit of his. He sat leaning slightly forward. He gave all the appearance that he might bolt and, at first, I was afraid he would escape from me as I endeavoured to drive the horse. After a few minutes riding, I realized that he was enjoying the experience. He would give a shudder or shake himself, in rhythm to the rattling of the carriage. Sometimes, he would make intricate motions with his hands, almost in sequence with the motion of the animal. He said nothing, but continued this excited jiggling for the entire journey. It reminded me of the Shakers that one reads about in New England. Perhaps deep religious ecstasy is to be gained from a buggy ride to Dartmouth?

~

The biggest revelation is his connection to music. He can sing many common songs as if he were the most gifted musician. However, his "singing" is not singing in the genuine sense as he does not understand the meaning; neither is he capable of extemporizing any part of a song. Occasionally, he will slur or drop a word, revealing his lack of understanding. The girl assigned primarily to his care takes great pride in having tutored him in several low ditties. She assures me he understands the words and will even use individual lyrics as a source of communication. I have yet to see this in action. If true, it would be a real advance in his treatment.

Ronan O'Driscoll

~

I have always considered myself a man of Science. I look around my commonplace surroundings and see all manner of things to improve. For example, there is the well they must trudge to every day for water. I explained to the Keeper of the farm this might be piped and a dynamo attached. I have read of such innovations in America. This would provide power and allow for the stringing of electrical lights, something unavailable in the entire area. The gains in self-sufficiency would be of significant benefit to the public purse. The Keeper said he would prefer more money from Council for housing the inmates. They do seem strapped for cash. I said I would speak to the relevant people about the matter.

~

In my opinion, the great opportunity of the case of the boy called Stewart is in advancing the new science of psychology. His inner life is a mystery for those of us with normal faculties. Imagine if we could understand whatever mechanism causes his strange condition. I think of the advances Dr. Alexander Bell has made on understanding the mechanism of the ear. Surely if we are this advanced in this organ, we are not far behind appreciating the mind itself? Dr. Bell spoke of Helen Keller being "chillingly empty" when he first met her as a dumb mute. Could not the same be said of Stewart? Keller was also wild as a savage before rehabilitation. Imagine if we could understand Stewart's condition and bring about a similar change? It would truly be a cause of celebration and put our efforts out here in provincial Nova Scotia on the world stage.

Dead house

Poor Farm, Cole Harbour, November, 1890

A fog rolled up from the estuary during the night. The temperature plummeted as the cold mist wound through the trees and bushes. By morning, it covered every bare branch in spiky hoarfrost.

The chill morning sun illuminated this transformed world. The fog departed; all that remained of it were skeins of mist on the open waters of the quiet bay—the corners of the shoreline already thin ice. A shimmering dust fell from the trees, not snow but ice crystals wafting down on the thin breeze. At certain angles, light caught on the gossamer mist and split into fleeting prisms.

The iron of the spade clanged as Hugh Morash dug into the stony soil. They could hear the plangent sound as far away as the farm buildings. Hugh cursed aloud as the sting of whatever stone he hit jarred him.

James Turner gave him a forbidding look. "'He who digs a pit will fall into it,'" he said wryly, quoting Proverbs. He didn't wish to scold Hugh too much, having him digging a grave this late in the year.

The younger man took a deep breath and leaned on the shovel, condensed breath clouding around his head. "Mr. Turner," he said, "I don't think I can dig this deep enough. Ground's too frozen."

After much deliberation, the Council had approved new staff over a year ago. Hugh had been the first hire, as farm labourer. He cursed and smoked clay pipes a lot. He had devious eyes and sometimes made lewd remarks to the female staff. He smirked at James and Eunice with a knowing smile.

James, strict Methodist, could not abide all this but kept his opinions to himself. He was getting too old for heavy work and needed the man's help. "Hmm," he said, scratching his beard. "She's been dead three days now. We have to bury her."

He looked around at the rocky area by the shore that they had picked for burials a few years back. Observing the white frost blurring the ground, he wondered how many bodies they had buried in the last three years. *Ten, was it?*

"Mightn't be so bad if we buried her up by the houses," Hugh suggested. "Soil hasn't frozen yet on the high ground."

James shook his head, coming out of his reverie. "No. Don't want to spook them. Besides, there's a history of burial down here."

He stood up from the remnant of a wall he had been sitting on. He grunted as he stretched, posterior numb from the cold stone. "A hundred years ago, pirates would pull in here and put the bodies of men in this spot for the winter."

"What, right there?" Hugh said, glad of the respite. "Looks like an old root cellar."

"Maybe," James mused, examining the mossy stone outline.

"Well, who said that?" Hugh asked after a while, irritated as always by the Keeper's tendency to lapse into silence.

"People around here," James said, straightening up. "I suppose we need to copy the pirates. Build a Dead House. I'll have to ask Council for more funds..."

He thought of how his brother-in-law would react to more requests for money.

"That won't help old Betty," Hugh said with a snicker. "Up there in her box behind the kitchen. We have to bury her somewhere."

James rubbed his hands together. The cold kept seeping into his woollen gloves. "Six dollars for the pine and black broadcloth," he mumbled, ending in a sigh.

"What about Betty's own box," Hugh jeered. "Wonder how many were in there." He liked to see how far he could push the old man.

James pretended not to hear. "Come on," he said, turning away. "Leave that spade there. We'll get Andrew and some more able-bodied ones. Bring her down here."

"What?" Hugh said. He glared at James's retreating back. "But the ground's too hard to dig. I told you."

"I know," James said, not looking back. His feet made black prints in the frost-covered grass. "We'll just have to cover her with those stones for the winter."

The Institute for the Deaf and Dumb

59 Maitland St, Halifax, November 16, 1890

Emmett toyed with his supper, his mind elsewhere. He had a starched collar on, and he kept moving his head unconsciously as it chafed him. From the other end of the dining room table, his mother observed him: the pallor of his cheeks and the customary black smudges under his eyes.

"Do you never sleep, Emmett?" she asked.

He looked around, as if suddenly realizing where he was. "Sleep?"

His mother made an exasperated sound. She fingered the cameo brooch at the throat of her high-necked blouse. It was a stylized portrait of Ophelia.

"You just look so tired and...dishevelled," she said. "Even dressed up smart like that. Like you never sleep."

"I do," he replied defensively. "I do sleep. This is just the way I look."

His mother made no reply, only turned to her own plate.

Angela interrupted the strained silence, appearing at the dining-room door, wiping her apron. "I've put the Reverend's dinner under a bowl in the pantry, Ma'am. He said he didn't know when he would make it home."

"Thank you, Angela," she said, giving her servant a significant look. Angela looked over at Emmett.

"What's this I hear about the poor farm?" she asked nonchalantly. "You working out there now?"

Emmett pushed some peas around his plate.

"As part of my duties," he said, not looking up. "I have to assess the progress of the inmates. There have been concerns about the operation of the farm."

"There many black folks out there?" she asked.

"A few." He nearly added "of course" but thought better of it.

"Hmm," Angela said. "You take care with those degenerates. If they wanted to work, they could."

"We put them to work," Emmett said. "Those that can. They don't just lie around. Some move on after a while. Some will never be able to. They're all types and from all over. Not just…coloureds."

"Huh," Angela said. She took off her apron and leaned into the kitchen to dispose of it. "I know my kind and how lazy they can be. I'll bet they can function well enough."

"Sit down, Angela," his mother offered, a prim dip of her jaw towards the empty chair. "Emmett has found one child, a boy he is making special efforts to help."

Emmett looked at his mother, then back to Angela. It was suddenly obvious they had been discussing him earlier.

He put down his fork and leaned back. "Hard to know how old he is." His tone was professional, sanctimonious. "Could be a teenager. Difficult to tell how his condition affects his growth. And he's lived rough for a while. Probably half st-st-starved. He's mute so we don't know how old he really is."

"Emmett," his mother said, "were he here, your father would tell you how proud he is. Helping these poor unfortunates. A very Christian thing to do, isn't it Angela?"

"Yes," Angela agreed in a dubious tone, observing him blush and squirm. "Is this boy safe from all the ruffians out there? A poor white boy like that isn't strong enough to look out for himself."

"Oh, it's not like that at all, at the farm. I've come to enjoy v-v-visiting since I've taken a special interest...in St-St-Stewart. That's his name...the name Sally gave him. Not sure why she picked it."

"Oh, Sally?" Angela said archly. "*Now* we see what's going on. Who's she, now?"

"She just works there," he replied defensively. "She's not related to him or anything."

He changed the topic. "We've even had a criminal attempt to claim him as her own. Now that he's been in the papers. Anyway, he never spoke until Sally took him walking one day. I believe she was singing some song: Irish or Scottish, whatever. We don't know if he's parroting her or if they mean something to him. Could be he really is of that background and he remembers songs from his childhood. It can't all have been unhappy..."

"Extraordinary!" Mrs. Forrestall exclaimed.

"It is," he agreed. "We think it possible to train him to speak like an ordinary person. That's why I'm off to this function tonight. At the Deaf and Dumb institute."

"So that's why I had to starch your collars," Angela said with disappointment. "Thought maybe you had a rendez-vous planned with this young lady. What's her name again?"

"Sally," his mother said, eyes sparkling. "Tell me, Emmett, what kind of family is she from?"

"I'm not...I hardly know her. She's not important...Just a scullery maid or something."

Angela blinked at this, hurt.

"Anyway, I'm not that hungry." He glanced up at the ornate carriage clock, a gift from the parish, on the mantle.

"I should be going. There will be quite a crowd, I'm sure. Bell has become world-famous."

"Angela, he means Alexander Graham *Bell*," his mother said. "To think our boy will meet this famous inventor and discuss such important matters. Whatever will you say to him?"

"Ask his opinion of the mute boy," Emmett mumbled through sudden, hurried bites. "Thinking of inviting him out to the farm. But who knows? Not even sure I'll get the chance to talk to him. Especially if I'm late."

He jumped up from the table, plate half-finished. He went to kiss Angela goodbye.

She fended him off, frowning. "You get out of here, Master Emmett. I'm done with your play-acting!"

"Goodnight, ladies," he announced with a laugh, rushing out the door. "Don't wait up, Mother."

His mother toyed with her brooch and stared at the carriage clock. She said nothing as Angela cleared away the plates.

"I'll be off myself," Angela said at last, knowing better than to discuss Emmett without invitation.

Mrs. Forrestall made no reply, not even a nod.

~

He skipped down the steps from their front door, out onto Maitland Street. The evening was damp and the view characteristically dull—a blend of fog and soot filling the air.

Emmett hated Halifax for its gloominess, especially on a night such as this: a gathering of important men of science! He refused to let the foreboding atmosphere affect his good mood.

Up steep Cornwallis Street, he passed the church Angela attended. The minuscule Coloured Baptist Church retreated from the scrutiny of a nearby gaslight street lamp.

He studied the shady facade, imagining all kinds of Voodoo ceremonies going on in there in the dark. Soon, he thought to himself, there would be electric lights here and along Gottingen. He turned right at the long street.

The plaintive howl of the steam-powered foghorn came up from the harbour below. As he strolled along, he reflected how often he heard its haunting tone but never saw the mechanical beast that made the strange wail. Like the destinations of the ships floating below, he has never been to any of the places they travelled to.

As he strolled, he listed out foreign ports he had only read about: London, Boston, New York, Barcelona, Alexandria, Istanbul, Tokyo. Imagine travelling to them all, a respected man of letters, consulted for his acumen at curing the mute. Honorary degrees, medals of honour, all would be heaped upon him. Just as they had done with Mr. Bell. Would the great man put a paternal hand on Emmett's shoulder and intone, "My boy, do call me Alec"?

He had to pause his fantasy to cross Gerrish Street. A constable bundled in his grey coat sauntered past down the hill.

The houses were meaner and more run-down the further along Gottingen you went. He passed the yard of the old carriage factory, strewn with half-fixed buggies, damaged wheels and other debris.

After a stretch of drab tenements leaning against each other, the street cleared to the grounds of the school. A four-columned portico fronted the two-storey building. Afflictions like deafness struck even the offspring of the wealthy on Tower Road, so this institute, founded thirty years ago on a "mean street" by a deaf Scottish tailor, flourished from generous donations.

The current Principal, George Tait, was also deaf and possessed great skill in securing funding from the parents of their wealthier charges. Events like tonight's demonstration by Mr. Bell ensured the continued prosperity of the institution. The advertisement in *The Morning Chronicle* promised Mr. Bell would speak on his progress on "Helping the Deaf to Hear". Tickets by invitation only.

Although he was early, Emmett was unsurprised to find a small queue at the school's entrance. After presenting his ticket, he followed the crowd to the lecture hall. a steep-sloped room, providing everyone a view of the speaker. Emmett walked down the steps, as near to the front as he could manage, and squeezed himself along the narrow seats.

He surveyed the crowd filling the vertiginous theatre —a sampling of the well-heeled of Halifax society: doctors, academics, bureaucrats, a smattering of reporters. He spotted a prominent politician sitting next to Dr. Reid from Dalhousie up front. Afterwards, he would use the opportunity to thank the Dean for his ticket as a ruse to talk to Bell.

There were plenty of ladies, some of them dressed as if for the annual ball at Province House. Emmett doubted most could absorb the learned discussion about to ensue.

He sat as straight as possible on the hard narrow bench, ignoring the older woman who sat beside him. He closed his eyes to listen to the babble of the crowd. It sounded like they were muttering a secret password repeatedly and couldn't help sharing it. Was it "*Barber*" or "*Rhubarb*" or "*Rather*"?

"Ladies and Gentlemen, welcome to the Institute of the Deaf and Dumb."

Emmett opened his eyes to see Principal Tait had reached the lectern and was beaming up at the assembly, causing a hush of expectation.

"It is my great pleasure to welcome tonight's distinguished guest to Halifax."

There was an awkward roundness to Tait's words. *He must be stone deaf*, Emmett marvelled.

Reading from notes, Tait glossed Bell's accomplishments. He described in detail the great man's work on behalf of the deaf. How even Bell's own wife was hard of hearing.

This surprised Emmett. *Funny how an ingenuity like the telephone could come out of a desire to help others hear.*

"Without further ado, would you please welcome a great champion for our cause and an honorary Nova Scotian, Doctor Alexander Graham Bell!"

Applause thundered as the inventor appeared from a side door and took to the lectern. He was tall and a little overweight, his curly hair and beard streaked with grey. His prominent eyes rolled, and he smiled in appreciation to the audience.

As he spoke, his enthusiasm reminded Emmett of a young boy, eager to please. "Why thank you so much, Principal Tait. And what a pleasure it is to be back in Nova Scotia. My next favourite province to the island of Cape Breton!"

A roar of laughter at the in-joke. Bell beamed, a clever schoolboy pleasing the entire class.

"Thank you. Thank you. Now, if you'll bear with me," his Scottish burr softened with a North American cadence, "I would like to speak about my recent exploration of what I call 'Oralism'. I have some transparencies here to share with you, using a projection device of my own devising."

An "Ooohh" from the audience as the lights dimmed. Then a glass plate illustrating a cross-section of the mouth and larynx was projected onto a screen behind Bell. This took some time to organize. The equipment was cumbersome and the operator unfamiliar with it.

Bell took it all in his stride, grinning good-humouredly at the learned gentlemen in the front row. "I hope my next invention isn't as difficult to operate as this one," he quipped.

The audience chuckled with admiration throughout the demonstration. They were as taken with the novelty of this celebrity and his magic-lantern as any of the technical descriptions of "Visible Speech" and Bell's ingenuous attempts at ensuring the deaf could pass as normal.

"In short, Ladies and Gentlemen, by the demonstrations and arguments I have laid out before you tonight. I hope I have demonstrated how any man afflicted with loss of their hearing may, by virtue of scientific advancement, one day communicate directly with his family and friends. There is no need for him to master a separate and awkward language of signs and so forth, necessarily distancing him from most men around him. Rather, he will have technologies such as the Photophone available to communicate clearly and directly with everyone."

There was a moment of silence before the gathered dignitaries of Halifax rose to applaud the conclusion.

Bell nodded and grinned, eyes twinkling as the clapping crescendoed and finally receded. He stood at the podium and raised his eyebrows expectantly at Tait—still putting his hands together with rapture.

The principal paused, glanced quickly at the expectant theatre behind him, then jumped up to stand beside the burly celebrity. "Thank you so much, Dr. Bell. Not only for tonight's remarkable presentation but also for all you have done to advance, not only our community, but society in general."

Vigorous bashful nodding from Bell.

"At this point, I would like to invite any members of the audience to ask any questions they might have of Dr. Bell."

Emmett leaped up. "What of those who can hear but do not speak?" His voice was reedy and petulant, an earnest student overanxious for approval.

"You are speaking of mutes," came Bell's rumbling reply.

"Yes, but those who can speak but do not," Emmett said. "I am aware of several cases. One in particular is very interesting."

Heads turned in his direction. Ladies' bonnets turned to each other, their owners whispering at his zealous tone. Academic lips pursed beneath bushy Victorian moustaches. Several eyebrows were raised.

"A fascinating topic, to be sure," the great man agreed. "My interest, due to my family situation as much as anything, has been to focus on those who can't speak because of lack of hearing."

He nodded to another hand at the middle of the hall.

"Did you fly down here from Cape Breton?"

A ripple of uncertain tittering from the crowd.

"Ah hah, no. I'm working on that too, though."

Emmett's heart sank. He wanted to ask more but couldn't form the question in an impressive enough way. He would just have to corner Bell in the reception later, despite having no official invite.

There followed an hour of questions. To Emmett's mind, most of them were gushing and inane, focused on stories about Bell in the popular press rather than about his research. The big man took it in his stride. If he thought the audience parochial compared to assemblies in Boston, London or Paris, he didn't let it show.

Finally, after what began as a question from one elderly lawyer but devolved into a rambling rumination about the unfairness of patent law, even Tait realized it was time to bring the evening to a close. Bell smiled at the old attorney who had stumbled to silence, and, ever the crowd-pleaser, simply answered "Yes."

Laughter all around the hall.

"Well," Tait said, "with that, I think this would be a good point to thank you all for coming and especially to thank the distinguished Doctor Bell for providing us with a remarkable night's entertainment. There will be a small reception for select guests in my chambers, but for everyone else, thank you again for your continued support of the Institute."

After the thunder of clapping died down, people stood and stretched, pleased to be free of the uncomfortable benches. Unlike before, when all the voices blended, Emmett heard individual exclamations of: "Splendid", "Remarkable", "A True Genius".

Tait ushered Bell off the stage, and a significant selection of the luminaries in the front rows followed. Emmett saw his chance and took it, stumbling out of his row past harrumphing men and disapproving ladies.

"Ah, Dean Reid. Good to see you again. I was particularly impressed with your question for Dr. Bell."

Reid's white beard hid his puzzled frown. He could not place this young man. "Ah, yes. Thank you. I...have we met?"

"Emmett Forrestall. With the Overseers. We collaborated on the design of the Poor Farm a few years back."

"Oh? We did. You're at Mitchener's office? I thought he'd be here tonight."

"Mr. Mitchener was indisposed this evening. I took his place."

Emmett didn't mention that his superior's indisposition resulted from Emmett not informing him of the invitation.

"Dr. Bell's ideas on Eugenics sound similar to your own," Emmett said quickly as the Dean pondered. "Have you corresponded?"

"Somewhat...I agree with his monogram upon the dangers of the formation of a deaf-mute version of humans. I find some of his resolutions problematic, however..."

"Mm-hmm," Emmett said. "Why don't we continue our discussion at the reception?"

"I suppose so..." Reid murmured, a trifle surprised at Emmett's urging by guiding his elbow towards the door. Emmett smiled thinly, suppressing his revulsion at the pungent odour of tobacco and orange the Dean emitted.

The principal's chambers were not big enough for the catered reception. Bodies pressed tightly into the two rooms, dimmed by an unaccustomed pall of smoke. A large quantity of this smoke spiralled up from the Tower Road tobacco king Tait was wooing for funding. They sat at his desk with a flustered junior assistant, frantically transcribing the conversation into his notebook.

A smattering of academics clustered together, like children in the schoolyard, pretending not to look over to the corner where Bell stood smiling and bowing to ladies.

Emmett detached from Reid and made a bee-line for Bell. "Mr. Bell, may I speak with you?"

"Absolutely! I remember your question. Intriguing."

Emmett interposed himself between a pair of ladies who left for elsewhere, trailing sour looks at his rudeness. "Thank you, sir. My name is Emmett Forrestall. I'm an Assessor for the County. I work with a Poor Farm for the Harmlessly Insane here in Halifax county. It's but a ferry ride across the harbour and a ride of an hour or so."

"Very good," Bell said, keeping his tone agreeable but looking around the room as if for a means of escape.

"The establishment takes in many types, hard cases and the like. May I say that I, in my small way, try to follow your example."

"Oh?"

"I consider myself a scientist. I have plans to build an electric dynamo there, powered by a water-wheel. It will be the first in the county! We'll have electric light out in the hinterland while everyone else is plunged in darkness."

"Well, that is remarkable. I believe I must—"

Sensing his listener's desire to move on, Emmett continued quickly. "I have one subject in particular whom you might find interesting. At first, we thought he was deaf-mute. Like your Helen Keller."

Bell's eyebrows raised. Despite himself, he paused his attempt at extraction.

"Turner, the Keeper, says they discovered the boy living savage. Worse than the lowest beast, eating at roots and mice. A farmer caught him trying to steal food. We think his parents abandoned him. He was most difficult in the beginning, but in recent months he has been civilized considerably. Through techniques I have developed."

Emmett took a breath. Bell saw an opportunity to interject.

"I...Well...That sounds most exceptional. I am extremely interested in the rehabilitation of the unfortunates of our society."

Emmett nodded. Pleased to have the great man's full attention. "Remarkable projections you showed tonight. I was st-st-struck by your explanation of the mechanism of the ear. How we can understand it as a machine, just like the telephone. I believe we can go further. Understand the mechanism of the brain. Fix it. Correct it. This boy I mentioned. He's not deaf. My experiments show that he can react to loud sounds. He's not mute, although his speech is garbled and almost impossible to understand. Do you recall the story of feral Peter, whom George the First kept and Swift wrote about? Perhaps you have heard of the savage found in Paris after the revolution?"

"Yes," ventured Bell, studying Emmett closely. "Perhaps I have."

"A Doctor Itard wrote of him. Rousseau's notion of the noble savage obsessed the man. The purity of the st-st-state of nature and civilization's corrupting influence. All that blather. We know better now, of course. The state of nature is...savage and cruel. However, I believe the child I have as my ward is like Itard's bête. I hope to st... st-st-study and improve him. I will publish my findings to the wider world."

"What a lot you have explained, sir," Bell said in his rumbling voice. "But surely this unfortunate child is a simpleton?"

"He is no common moron. Although we have those aplenty at the farm. He possesses an animal cunning. It is my belief that his mind holds the key to the tumult in society. If we could civilize this child, then could we not do the same with all the lesser orders: criminals, the racially inferior, and so on. Perhaps a gentleman of such renown as Alexander Graham Bell would lend his name to my endeavour?"

Bell blinked his heavy eyelids. He received these offers regularly in America. He didn't expect such in Nova Scotia. "You want to be famous?" he rumbled. "A celebrated genius. Like me, perhaps? Y'know, I accomplished nothing without the help of those around me. My father with his care for the deaf. That's what inspired me to the telephone. Important to remember that—"

"I have had a lot of help from the staff at the farm." Emmett did his best to sound chastened.

"Very good," Bell said. "Do you have a calling card? Mister..."

"Forrestall." Emmett had prepared for this and fished the carefully produced card from his waistcoat. "Here you are, sir. Perhaps you will come to the farm and pay us a v-v-visit."

"I am engaged to travel to Montreal tomorrow and then on to the United States. However, I will keep you in mind. Perhaps you could write a detailed report and send it to me?"

"Definitely! I have taken extensive notes and would be happy to collate a report."

Dean Reid bustled over to question the great man, drawing him away from the frowning Emmett. Bell nodded absent-mindedly, perhaps glad of the rescue.

Emmett considered joining the conversation, but an acute glare from Reid warned him off. The rush of speaking for so long and the stuffy room made Emmett feel dizzy. He took his leave, planning his report.

He was outside in the cool November drizzle when he realized that the celebrated inventor had not shared his own calling card.

Cuckoo

Poor Farm, Cole Harbour, December, 1890

Sally put down her brush, giving up on trying to tame her frizzy hair. It was tiresome to have it up all the time, with all the work to be done. Perhaps, she reflected, she could sell it. There were hairdressers who would buy it for wigs. Better to have as much money as she can before... Before *what?*

She sighed at her reflection in the speckled mirror, and pulled the hair back in a tail. Perhaps she could pass as a man? She would have to wear a jacket, for her chest wasn't flat enough.

She blew her cheeks out in exasperation. The candle in the little privy flickered. There was barely enough room to turn in here: a chipped enamel chamber pot, a ledge beneath the mirror for a little basin and a cracked jug. No lock on the door.

Sally saw the louse crawling over of her scalp, tightened her lips as she pursued it. "Got you, little bug-ger."

Must have got them off Stewart. She had spent an hour today attempting to tame the wild shrub of his hair. He hated the scissors and got agitated when she approached with it. Andrew wanted to hold him down while they cut it, but she had prevailed. She promised she would do it while he slept.

Feeling about for other lice, she pondered the problem of Stewart. Could she really leave him here? But how could she bring him with her? He had improved a lot recently: she had him in the kitchen, putting cleaned cutlery in the drawer. This had gleaned much praise from Matron.

He would improve with time. Besides, he wasn't *her* Stewart. They wouldn't tell her where her baby was taken, but the rumour was the nuns sent children to rich families in Boston.

She touched the hem of her skirt. The folded notes she kept sewed in there.

She felt the pull south like the migratory geese, a ley line that couldn't be seen, but she felt it all the same. She had seen a V of them flying overhead at dusk and took it as a sign.

"Birds can tell you the future," her Nan had said, as they watched a flock form and reform. *But what did those impossible shapes mean?*

Nan had been the only one on her side. Gave her some money to leave the Island and flee down to Halifax. Nan had pressed the brush and the tortoiseshell comb into her hands as a parting gift. The old woman was always stern, so the tears in her eyes were a shock. They held each other fiercely before Sally tore herself away. Almost as fiercely as she had held the true Stewart the last time.

Sally squatted over the chamber pot and relieved herself. The urine rattled against the pot with a melodic ring. *There was almost a tune to it.*

She hummed something she had heard today. Was it Ned who had been humming it? He was such a sweet singer. What a shame about his deformed mouth. He was quite attractive otherwise. Or had it been Stewart's tune?

Thinking about birds and tunes, she realized Stewart reminded her of a cuckoo. Can't they copy any other bird's tune if they want? The eggs they laid were said to change colour to match the others in the nest. She remembered the robin's eggshell they spotted the day he first sang. *Perhaps he's a cuckoo pushing her true Stewart out of her heart?*

A distant clatter and raised voices put an abrupt end to Sally's pondering. She ripped a strip of newspaper to wipe herself clean and pulled up her undergarment. "...police are waging war against the cattle that are allowed to roam at large to the destruction of the Park. The Chief has already impounded fourteen. Dartmouth..."

She affixed the comb to her hair. Strands spilled every-where, but it would keep the bulk of it up—an attempt at decorum. She grabbed her brush and candle and slipped out of the narrow privy.

Sally followed the sounds upstairs. Jenny in her night-dress was at the head of a cluster of inmates. She thrust her prominent jaw forward, giving her a bulldog appear-ance. The gang stood outside one of the smaller rooms, where a banging and wailing emanated. Neither Matron nor Keeper were anywhere to be seen.

"What's all this racket?" Sally asked.

"Him! *Of course.* That bastard has the run of this place." Jenny was beside herself with anger. "Woke us all up."

"Who? Stewart?" Sally peered past to the room within.

Stewart was rocking himself back and forth in his nar-row cot. His motions had a jerky sameness to them, like an animal caught in a trap.

Sally wondered at his behaviour. She had seen him up-set before, but his wailing and rocking was so persistent that he looked like he would injure himself. She wondered if someone had threatened violence on him.

Poor thing, she thought, he must be frozen without a blanket. I'm half frozen myself.

"Awwww. Ooooh. Aawwwww."

"Shut up, stupid kid," Jenny growled, "or I'll give you something to moan about."

"Awwwwww. Oooooooh. Aaaawwwww."

"Leave him alone. He can't help it."

"What do you know, Sally? You a nurse or something, now?"

"I know you're a fool, Jenny White."

"Oh, yes. A strumpet like you don't get to call me anything. I'll come over there and sort you out, so I will."

"Shut up, the two of you," old Nora said. "You're making him worse."

Jenny walked into the little room. She put her face right next to Stewart's. "You shut it, or I will hurt you. So help me."

He started moaning louder now, covering his ears.

Jenny pulled back, frightened by his response.

"Jenny, get away from him," Sally said. "I'll sort you out proper if I have to."

Jenny stood up, calculating. There was nothing she would gain from more belligerence. She adjusted the faded bonnet on her chin. They made the women inmates wear them at night. "Why don't you get into bed with him, then. You want to mind him so much."

"All right," said Sally. "I will."

Sally felt Jenny's shock in the dim light. She slipped across the frozen pine floor. Approaching his bed, she set the candle on the ground. Stewart's body was tense. She put a hand on his thin shoulders to stop his rocking. He shied away from her touch as if from fire.

"Shush now, Stewart. We all want to sleep. You're making too much noise. You have to stop or they'll put you out in the Violents' room or something terrible."

By some miracle, he slowed. She lay on the bed along-side him. Incredulous, Jenny and the rest left, with much whispered cursing.

Sally stayed beside him, stroking his bony back. All night long he kept up a low moaning.

She eventually fell asleep, her hand resting against his spine.

The Halifax Club

Hollis Street, Halifax, January, 1891

Emmett shook snow from his black twill overcoat, a birthday gift from his mother now that he was "making a name for himself" and needed to look more presentable.

The maître'd's mouth formed a moue of distaste as the wet snow pooled on the black and white tile of the ornate foyer. The severe pattern of black Xs within white squares caused Emmett to blink.

"May I be of assistance?" the maître'd murmured, stirring from behind his little desk. "Are you expected?"

"Yes. I am."

Emmett took in the ornate white-and-gilded mouldings of the room, the sweep of the plush carpeted staircase, the oil paintings of pastoral provincial scenes. The glittering chandeliers. He spotted an imposing painting of Richard John Uniacke, the famous ancestor of the club's founder. Didn't he, thought Emmett, dream up Confederation decades before anyone else? *Wasn't he from Ireland too?*

"Excuse me," the maître'd said.

"Mr. Mitchener," Emmett declared, enjoying the changed look on the man's features. "He's expecting me. Emmett Forrestall."

"Yes. I have your name here," came the smooth reply. "Right this way."

Uniacke stared down with skepticism as Emmett walked past on his way to the lounge upstairs. Large picture windows looked out on Hollis Street. Gentlemen reclined on stuffed leather chairs dotting the room, light streaming in shafts through the clouds of their tobacco smoke. A grand piano rested heavily in one corner beside a mahogany fireplace.

"Emmett," Mitchener intoned. He rose from his chair, gesturing with his pipe towards a side room. The shoulders of his dark jacket were dusted with a mix of ash and dandruff. "We can meet in one of the private rooms. Don't want to disturb…the other fellows."

If anyone else looked disturbed, they didn't show it. Emmett was struck by their resemblance to the inmates in the poor farm, sitting around.

He nodded and followed his superior through an annex to an adjoining room. The room looked out onto a courtyard in the middle of the building. Emmett admired the little garden while Mitchener closed the door, easing his bulk behind the table facing him. A painting of a ship firing its cannons adorned the opposite wall. HMS *Shannon*, Emmett supposed.

"You might as well sit," Mitchener grunted, "although this won't take too long."

Emmett sank down onto an ornate dining chair. He wondered if it was to be some kind of promotion or perhaps a reassignment to another department. He unsuccessfully tried to keep a smirk off his face. He would insist on a salary increase.

"I'm afraid we're going to have to let you go."

At about seven years old, Emmett had crept up the roof of Saint George's and crawled to the comet-topped cupola at the peak. Once there, he looked down—a vertiginous fall out of the sky into the harbour below. He froze, unable to move. It was some time before one of his father's parishioners spotted him and raised the alarm. His stomach lurched with the same sensation of falling.

"Wha—What? I don't understand. My father will—"

"Your father will *what*?" Mitchener interrupted. "I wouldn't be relying too much on his influence. When he hears—"

"What did I do?"

"This business with Bell." Mitchener made a disgusted noise. "What were you thinking? Propositioning an important thinker with some mad-cap scheme. Inviting him out to the Poor Farm. Don't you know what that place is for?"

"I...I was trying to help—"

"Exactly! There's no helping anyone out there. That's why they're there. When Dr. Reid told me you had gone to the Deaf and Dumb Institute under my name and done that..." Mitchener glared at him.

"I'm sorry. You weren't in the office. I thought you wouldn't be interested—"

"Not interested? The best of Halifax were there that night! Watching you, as a representative of my department, asking crackpot questions of a visiting dignitary."

Emmett swallowed, remembering the stares from the audience. They had recognized him. Halifax was a very small place.

"And what is all this carry-on out in Cole Harbour? Experiments? Therapies?" The colour in Mitchener's face grew puce as his voice rose with anger. "With some moron child? There are already questions around the Keeper out there. He let you continue with this?"

"It wasn't the Keeper," Emmett said, surprised he was defending James Turner.

"It's his job to keep the place well run! Now it seems a couple of the papers have gotten wind of this boy. His mother came to our office and you deliberately turned her away. What if the papers got hold of *that*? I'll be directing your replacement to ensure we restore him to her."

"But she's a fake," Emmett said. "A charlatan. She only wants to make money off St-st-ste—"

He struggled for too long on the name. Mitchener eyed him with contempt.

"Oh Ste-Ste-Stewart. You can't even say it! What a useless article you are. Perhaps you should apply to be an inmate out there, now you're done. I've never before had such an ignoramus in my office. I wouldn't go looking for another job in this town too soon. Halifax is as small as this club and plenty will know of your dismissal. I've already informed your father about the matter."

Emmett bowed his head. He felt like the older man had reached into his chest and snapped something. Tears stood in his eyes.

"Why here?" he asked, voice tearful. "Why'd you bring me here?"

"The club?" Mitchener leaned back. "Didn't want you making another scene back at the office. They have a guard on staff here, should you get any notions."

"My desk. My things?"

"Arthur has already cleared it out. Whatever was yours will be delivered to your parents'."

A cold clarity came over Emmett. He took a deep breath. "What will happen to... St-St-Stewart?"

"That's not your concern anymore." Mitchener arched an eyebrow. "You *are* an odd one, Forrestall. What was it that made you throw everything away on this whore's imbecile son?"

"He's not..." Emmett found he couldn't say any more. He sat there and wiped his eyes.

Mitchener let a whole minute pass before saying with finality, "Leave now. My advice is you put all this behind you. Leave."

Emmett's nod was meek. He hurried out of the ornate building, never to return.

~

Emmett stumbled home. The snowy morning had turned mild, and the streets were slick and soft from melting snow. He had spoiled his best shoes. Tradesmen driving carts, soldiers, stray dogs, even the Town Clock on Citadel Hill stared at him as he walked by. He was incandescent with shame. Surely everyone saw it.

Should he kill himself? Which was better: drown in the harbour or jump from the church roof? The latter would be a dramatic enough gesture, surely. Halifax would never forget him after that. Didn't he want to be famous? Not to be forgotten? But the high church roof still terrified him: a terror as visceral as this morning's dismissal.

Consequences haunted him at each street corner. He wouldn't be consulting with Alexander Graham Bell or Dr. Reid; there would be no touring of Stewart to appreciative audiences; no interviews in learned journals, or even newspapers. Each shock of truth hit with the force of a punch to his stomach.

When he finally reached Maitland Street, he fumbled with the front door for a long time. Perhaps, he reasoned, he could race upstairs to his room and end himself there before anybody saw him. He supposed he could make a noose from a curtain tieback. Would that tasselled thing hold?

"Emmett," his mother called from the front parlour. "Come sit down."

Her voice was icy calm, cold as the wind off the harbour.

Emmett staggered into the room, collapsing into a chair. "Is father home?" was all he could manage.

She rolled her reddened eyes up to heaven. "He's out. He told me everything. He didn't want to see you. I dismissed Angela, too."

That did it. Emmett's sobs heaved out of him, a violent physical reaction akin to vomiting. He said words, even phrases, disjointed and meaningless: "unfair", "didn't know" and "blasted poor farm". It took a good ten minutes before he ran out of energy. She did not go to him.

He finally finished railing and looked at her quizzically.

"Are you done?" she asked.

He gaped at her, having never heard this tone before.

"This kind of behaviour is unacceptable." She took a deep breath and spoke in a monotone to the wall above him. "We've decided that you can no longer live here. The damage to your father's reputation is too great. You will pack tonight and leave tomorrow on the steamer for Belfast. We'll write to your cousin and arrange...something for when you get there. Harold has connections at the Assembly Seminary. Perhaps, *if* you promise to quietly finish your studies and get your divinity degree, we'll pay for that. Ourselves. Otherwise, you are on your own. We are very disappointed in you, Emmett, but you're our son. What do you say?"

Her face was pale and her eyes glistened, but her voice remained firm as she delivered his sentence. For the first time, he realized his mother had aged; she was an older woman.

He couldn't think what to say. He meekly nodded and retreated to his attic room.

He planned on ending his life that night. He would have liked to punish his parents with suicide.

Instead, he packed his notes, books and clothes into the battered case left on his bed and went to the steamer the next day. From the frigid deck, he watched Halifax disappear into the dusk until it was no more than a smudge on the horizon.

Lion and Bright

Poor Farm, Cole Harbour, Spring 1891

Smoke rose above the distant field. George Bissett grimaced at it. The Poor Farm was a fair distance over there from his place, he brooded, through a swampy bit of woods.

There was never any harm in keeping an eye on James, though. In George's opinion, all James did was lie around idle while the inmates ran wild. And then he had the gall to ask Council for more funds. George felt for the letter in his jacket. He had to deliver this, too.

George groused to himself all the while as he trudged to visit his brother-in-law: his back was stiff from the change in the weather; he never had enough time for his own farm with all the Council work.

George liked to dwell on perceived wrongs. He enjoyed having them fester, poking at them and making them worse. What he saw as James's blame for the doomed dyke project was a favourite. And then his own wife had insisted George make James Keeper—the softest job outside of Halifax!

George had to pause and shake his head, steadying himself with a hand against a tall silver birch. He could see across to men in the clearing. Many were standing around, staring into the bonfire of trees they had cleared.

Jesus! If the position was George's, he would show them. He'd have every one of those lazy bastards working flat out. He would scream at how useless they were if they gave any resistance. Could he get away with whipping them?

He fantasized about it: he had enough Council connections. Finally, proper work would get done at this farm.

He walked down the hill towards the group, grinding his teeth all the while. A stolid ox was hitched to a stump at the top of the field. Hugh Morash was having trouble convincing the creature to move.

"Hello, Mr. Bissett," Hugh called. "Looking for the Keeper?"

"Yes. Where is he?" George's words came out clipped.

"What's that, sir? Here, I'll bring you down to him. Give old Lion a rest. He doesn't want to do much today, anyway."

George made no response, only pursed his lips.

Hugh unhitched the beast and left it to graze on the patchy ground.

"Where's the other ox?" George said. "Didn't you get a pair?"

Hugh clicked his tongue. "Bright was part of the Easter celebrations. Although he didn't taste too good."

George glowered at him, not appreciating his flippant tone.

"This way," said Hugh mildly. "I expect Keeper's down by the fire."

They picked their way down through the rocky field, George fuming all the while. The bonfire crackled and roared as they came near. Its heat was so strong no one came too close. Tongues of flame licked ravenously on the marrow of felled trees.

The men sat on rocks and hillocks, mesmerized by the sight. James stood as his brother-in-law drew near.

"Sorry to disturb you," George said, tucking away his anger so he could dole it out later. "Don't want to upset your work."

"S'alright," James said, wiping his forehead with a handkerchief.

George knew better than to wait for pleasantries from his brother-in-law. "You're a long time clearing this field." He surveyed the quiet group around them. "Lucky for you there are more inmates coming. To help you out. Mount Hope's full to the rafters."

The other men raised eyebrows and exchanged glances, straining to hear.

"More?" James said. "We're full here, too."

George shrugged, pleased at the troubled look on the Keeper's face. "We're putting out a tender for more dormitories. Probably be John Wilson again. After all, he did the first ones."

"Wilson? He's a terrible carpenter. That stable barn he put up over the winter is coming to pieces already."

"Barn? What barn?" George cursed inaudibly. "No one authorized that."

Sparks crackled and leapt into the air as the two men stared at each other.

"Never mind," George said. "I'll talk to Bertie Wilson. Chairman Wilson. You'll have to take me to see this barn."

James made a noncommittal gesture.

"New buildings, is it?" Hugh said, hovering on the edge of the conversation. "This lot don't know how lucky they are. To be getting more fine hotel rooms!"

Jean Paul and other nearby inmates chuckled sarcastically.

George ignored them. He took the envelope from his pocket. "Before I forget. Release form. Seamus Mulvaney.

Is he here?" He looked around at the assembled workers. "Where is he?"

"We don't have any Seamus Mulvaney," James said.

"He's about thirteen, according to his mother. Shouldn't he be out working?"

"If I may," Hugh said with a smirk, "I believe Mr. Bissett means Stewart."

James's brow creased with confusion. "Stewart? He's an orphan. And Eunice wants him...for other work. How do you know this other name for him, Hugh Morash?"

"Me? Oh, just something I heard. An acquaintance in Irishtown. I believe she has a claim on our singing star—"

"Singing?" George said. "What is this now?"

"Stewart," Hugh said, voice silky, "was mute but now can sing."

George goggle-eyed James. "*Sing?*"

"It was Eunice's idea." James heaved a sigh and looked into the flames.

This was too much. "You are the Keeper!" George said. "If it gets out we are teaching them to sing and not putting them to work..." He glared at the surrounding men, raising his voice. "You lot! Get to work now. No more lounging around, listening to your betters."

The men made themselves scarce. They were used to unwarranted abuse. Best to get out of range of it.

"I'll take them back up the field," Hugh said, delight in his voice. He lunged forward, cuffing one man hard. "C'mon you black bastard, you heard the Squire. Things are changing around here. Up and work on that stump."

James only nodded at Hugh's display. He turned away and started walking towards the farmhouses, Stewart's release envelope in hand.

George, incensed by Hugh's calling him by his nick-name, marched beside him, growling invectives all the way at how the farm was run.

~

Eunice watched out the window with foreboding as her husband marched around the building to the front door, followed closely by his sister's haranguing husband. She ordered Jenny to move any inmates into the dining hall early, then hurried to meet the men.

"George!" she exclaimed. "Did something happen in the high field?"

George regarded her, temper cooling. He didn't want her complaining too much to Sophia. They were thick as sisters, although Sophia was actually James's sister.

He composed his features, keeping his voice bland and even. "Eunice. Just discussing business with James. Nothing for you to worry about."

"Your 'discussion' sounded pretty heated."

Eunice looked to James for clarity. His face was closed, betraying nothing.

"Go through to the office," he grunted.

Eunice noted the envelope in his hand and led them across the narrow hall. She let the men go in, then stepped into the room, closing the door behind her.

Worry racked her. *Were they to be let go?* Surely George would protect them. The accusations were mostly untrue, she reflected, but James might have bought some more things without telling her.

George settled into the biggest chair and smiled. His smile was thin and humourless. "Sit down, Eunice. Everything going well? Sophia told me to ask after you."

She frowned, sinking into the chair by the door. James ignored the banter and looked up from the official letter.

"Stewart," he said. "Real name's Seamus. Seamus Mulvaney. Mother in Dartmouth is claiming him."

"Stewart? Is she legitimate?" Consternation mixed with relief in her voice. *This was all about the child.*

"Legitimate?" There was savour in George's voice. "Overseers say so. We can't be indulging in this foolishness about teaching him to speak or sing. That's not how we are to do things."

There's the real George, Eunice thought.

"But Emmett...Mr. Forrestall. He gave us his support."

"Oh, that piece of work," George said. "I heard about *him*. They sent him packing. Back to Ireland. Caught doing all kinds of improper business at the Overseers'. So he's off to be clergy for the natives outside Belfast."

"I warned you," James said solemnly. "This scheme with the boy was a bad idea."

"Scheme?" Eunice hated how shrill her voice got when her emotions ran high. "I was only trying to improve things out here. What they are saying about how we run things. I wanted to—"

George laughed. "Is that what this is all about? Don't you worry, Eunice. Leave the politics to me. And keep a better hand on your husband. We've been discussing it and things are going to change out here."

"What about the boy?"

"We're to bring him back tomorrow." James said, unable to look at her. "It will be the start of doing things properly out here."

George leaned back with a satisfied smile at Eunice. Disgusted, she stood up and left the room.

~

"He's going. That's all there is to it."

Sally gazed in disbelief at the Matron. They were in the kitchen, lines of large pots simmered about them. The windows sweated with condensation. Eunice had told the other staff to wait outside "briefly".

Sally noted Eunice's paleness and the redness of her eyes. *Had she been crying?* "Matron, we can't let them take him. Who is this person? If she's really his mother, how did she let him go in the first place? Why come for him now? And what about Emmett? He was telling us to keep teaching him. Helping us."

"Mr. Forrestall is no longer with the Overseers. He's left the province." Eunice's tone was firm now.

Sally did a double-take at that. *Was it connected?* "But...Stewart's been doing so much better since...since we started helping him. He's calmer and...saying words."

Sally heard her her speech as from outside herself. Cold shock overtook her, as if someone was pushing her into deep water.

"I know you're fond of him," Eunice said. She took out a handkerchief and quietly wiped her eyes. "I blame myself. I shouldn't have let you get so close. They want to change the farm. Harden how we run things."

"They don't want us to help people?" Sally's voice was shrill. "What is wrong with these people in control? And they're just going to hand over our best example to someone pretending to be his mother?"

Eunice put away the handkerchief, coming to a resolution. "Sally. That's enough. I want you to help prepare him tomorrow. He trusts you. Help us get him into Dartmouth without too much fuss."

"I'm not—What you're asking is..." Sally backed away. "I can't do that."

"It's not a choice." Eunice's mouth settled into a firm line. "As a servant here, you do what we tell you. Otherwise you may reconsider your position. Now. Go out and bring the rest back in. We've a meal to prepare."

Sally looked about, disbelief warring with anger. "But… Eunice. We can't—"

"That is all. Do as you're told."

Sally stilled, resentment plain on her features. She bowed her head and walked out, noting that one of the pot lids was rattling angrily. *How appropriate.*

Double Vision

Poor Farm, Cole Harbour, Spring 1891

As she lay in bed that night, Sally's mind jumped about, unable to settle on anything. *"Like a hen on a hot griddle."* Another saying of grandmother's.

What had it been like for her? Leaving Ireland for this unknown place. She sometimes told Sally stories of the crossing: the terrible food, the misery of the coffin ship.

A half-moon dimly lit Sally's narrow room of bare pine walls. *My own coffin.*

In the bed beside hers, Esther snored softly. Esther helped in the kitchen mostly and didn't bother Sally much. Sally suspected she was afraid of her. She might not even raise the alarm if she woke and found Sally gone.

Sally propped herself up on her elbows. No more waiting. The time to go was now. She knew the doors were all locked once curfew came. None of the windows opened enough either. But she knew where Eunice kept a spare key in the office. In case of fire. The staff quarters were near the office, too.

Sally was sure she wouldn't make any noise, but what about Stewart? She sighed. *I can't take him, can I?* Who knew what kind of life he would have: given away to some confidence artist.

She recalled his smile when they sang and an idea came to her. She convinced herself the plan would work.

In the dim light, she felt about for her clothes. The floorboards creaked and Esther grumbled, turning over. Sally held her breath, waiting for discovery. No response.

She reached under the bed for a battered carpet bag. She had filled it after supper with everything she could filch. It would have been better to wait until she had more money, but there was no choice now.

Out into the hall. Another agony of waiting after the door creaked closed. No sound from Esther. No yelling out. Sally relaxed a fraction.

She listened to a hush in the hallway that made her pause, realizing it was the sound of everyone asleep. She had never noticed it before. A mouse scampered along the wainscotting. Sally wished them both good luck.

She made so much noise on the rickety stairs; she was certain someone would discover her. She had the foresight to leave her bag by the front door before crossing to the Keeper's office.

The door didn't open at first. Maybe the Keeper locked it at night? She tried again, and it yielded.

Deep breath. Into the room she crept, hunting around in the dark for the key. Did she dare risk lighting a lamp? She felt along the shelves. Nothing. She tried the little nooks in the Keeper's rolltop desk, stuffed with dockets and invoices.

A sharp pain. She had to bite down on her lip to stop herself yelling. The syringe. *Christ!* What if she had drugged herself? She sat down for a moment, breathing heavily. If they caught her, she'd probably be arrested. Sent to Rockhead.

Amid all the worry, she remembered meeting here with Stewart and Emmett. Most of his "experiments" were foolish. Anything that might have harmed Stewart, she had put a stop to. She briefly wondered where Emmett had gone. No doubt he had already forgotten them.

She tried taking deep breaths, as he had instructed Stewart, to calm herself. The memory of Emmett taking the key off the top shelf came in a flash. He used to lock them into the room.

She thanked his paranoia and reached up, grabbing a handful of keys. If there ever was a fire, she thought, they would be a long time unlocking the doors.

Back out into the hall and through the enclosed walkway to the men's quarters. She would have to be extra careful. There was no straightforward explanation if they caught her here at this hour. She might claim to be helping Stewart, but he hadn't been calling out. And why was she dressed?

Someone was moaning in the main dormitory. She supposed one or two of them made noise through most of the night—cover for any accidental racket she might make. Stewart was still in his own room, the door closed. She sneaked in, sensing more than seeing his indistinct form. She crouched near him, putting the keys beside the bed. This would not be easy.

"Stewart? Wake up, my pet."

He groused a bit, turning away from her. She thought about stirring him some more before she remembered her plan.

She went back to the door, closing it softly. Back to the bedside, she stroked his hair. She whisper-sang his favourite lines from their first song:

> He dreamed that he was walking
> > far down by the ocean side,
> And saw his true love floating
> > down on the silvery tide.

She only sang the same two verses, over and over. Eventually, he turned to toward her. "The sibbery tide?"

"Shush! Yes, Stewart. Do you want to come with me, down to the Silvery Tide?"

He sat up. Her eyes were used to the dark by now and she spotted where he had piled his clothes.

"Come on," she entreated. "Let's get you dressed."

He started a low uncertain groan, distressed by this change of routine.

"Shhh! Here. Sing with me..."

She started the song all over, waiting for him to follow. Uncertainly, he joined in. Slowly, she got him into his clothes.

"All right, then. Keep singing. Just hold my hand and we'll slip downstairs, quiet as mice."

He said nothing but took her hand.

It was an eternity to the stairs. She heard someone call out from the dormitory and Sally froze. *Should they run?* Someone shushed whoever yelled out, and she whispered the single phrase "down on the silvery tide."

She heard him chortle a little before repeating the words. At least, she thought, someone thinks it's funny.

They crept down the stairs, through to the Centre Wing and up to the front door. Her bag was still there.

Sally's heart sank. *The keys.* She had left them up in his room. She nearly cursed aloud. A fear overcame Sally: a sense of someone in the hall with them. She stared into the darkness but only saw a ghostly shape she took for moonlight.

Stewart was shifting from foot to foot. She panicked. She couldn't leave him here. Who knew what noise he would make.

In desperation, she tried the big iron latch.

It opened.

What? She couldn't believe her luck. The Keeper must have forgotten to lock it.

She looked out. Nothing stirred and the half moon had risen. It was clear enough to see to the trees. This was madness. How long was it going to take to get out of the countryside? Surely they would be spotted. Search parties sent. The word would be out, looking for them. Even bears and wolves were about this time of year.

"C'mon, Stewart. Now's our chance."

With a small laugh, he followed Sally out into the darkness.

~

The trill of the screech owl's cry made Sally jump. She paused, Stewart's hand held tight. He had followed her without too much opposition, stumbling half asleep.

She worried about what he would be like when it brightened and he got hungry. The poor farm porridge often made you queasy, but it still filled your belly. She had some cheese. How long would that last?

They cleared the bright, open fields running and were into the woods. The wind had picked up, and the moonlight didn't provide so much light through the trees.

"Why don't we take a breather?" Sally said. She got him to sit down on a log beside her.

Never having expected to get this far, she needed to think through the next steps: get to town, then figure out the best way out of town without drawing too much attention.

She had enough for a train to Yarmouth. Could she get a ship from there? She had heard there were lots of Bluenosers in Quincy, Massachusetts. Maybe someone might take pity on them and help them onto the steamer.

A branch snapped.

Both froze as if it had been lightning. Wolf? They held onto each other in the dark. *Was that a light?*

Stewart cried out: a groan of fear.

Then Sally heard the laugh. Hugh hurried towards them, his lantern filling the clearing.

"Lost you there for a bit," he chuckled. He had a large cudgel in his other hand.

"What do you want?" Sally snarled. She went to face him.

"Stay there," he said. "I know how dangerous you are."

He put the lantern on the ground. It opened a globe of light in the dark woods. The glow exaggerated his features.

He held his club aloft, facing them. "Here we are! Going for a midnight picnic, are we?"

"It's none of your business."

"That's where you're wrong." Hugh edged closer. He seemed to loom over them. "I planned all this. Mulvaney is an old whore down in Irishtown. I put her up to being Stewart's mother."

He grabbed Stewart by the jaw and spoke menacingly into his face. "Huh, Seamus? Do you like that touch? I told her to call you the most stupid name possible. The old biddy agreed, thinking there might be money in it."

"Leave him be!" Sally pushed out at Hugh.

He was ready this time and swung the club, glancing the side of her head. She dropped to the ground, dazed.

Hugh gave a satisfied chuckle, grabbing Stewart again. "See that? Your precious Sally ain't so smart now. She'd never have got you out, anyway. Who do you think left the door unlocked? I was watching you the whole time."

Sally felt at her head, sparks of light clouding her vision. She struggled to form words. "Hugh. Listen, just let us go. I'll tell them what you said. About...everything."

His laugh was triumphant. "Do you think they'll listen to you? Do you think they *care*? Squire Bissett was laying down the law for Turner just this morning. They'd listen to this miracle mute before *you*. No, here's what'll happen. We're going to have a bit of fun while 'Seamus' watches. Then I'll bring you both back. Sheep back into the pen." In the lamplight, his eyes glowed with anticipation.

Sally tried to hit out at him but something was wrong with her balance. She stumbled forward, falling hard on the undergrowth.

In the dim light, Sally saw Hugh unbutton his trousers. In her daze, it looked like there was two of everything.

"Now," Hugh's voice was an animal growl, "time for Stewart to see what it means to be a man."

His words echoed in Sally's ears. She looked to Stewart, seeing two of him.

~

You want to run off. You could make noises to cover Sally's screaming, as you did when your father would hit your mother. When he came home with that awful smell. At first, he was all sweet soft words, a gentle slur to his speech. Then, out of nowhere, he would just hit her. You hated it, but there was nothing you could do.

You could run away. Down to the water. You could crash through the bushes and branches, never looking back. Sally said you were going to the Silvery Tide. Into the water. She would be out there, wouldn't she? Out there on the tide.

But you know he means her harm. So you run at him. You shout and yell, thrashing and flailing. You remember the man in the Stained Glass, so hurt and holy. He had a beard, too. You smash the glass to get at him.

Hugh pulls back in surprise, trousers half-down. Sally takes the chance and grabs the club.

Distracted by you, Hugh turns back toward her too late. She belts him in the side. He falls back, eyes rolling with fear.

"I'll tell you what to tell them," Sally says, standing shakily. "Tell them a girl and a mute beat you."

He cowers, covering his face as she swings the cudgel, knocking him cold.

She reaches out to you, but you run away, into the darkness. This is all too much. You need to run. Brambles tear at your feet and hands, slowing you down. You stop and hide.

She calls out, a teary sound in her voice. You say nothing. It is the only safe way.

Her voice goes quiet. *Is she gone?*

Then she reaches out and pats your back. "Shush now, Stewart, my love. We're going to get out of here. I promise you. But you have to help."

You let her hold you. For a few moments.

The next parts are a blur.

You make it through the night. The next day, you hide. You even sing together a bit and are happy.

Once, men with sticks come near, hollering to each other. But you stay still as stones, only your hearts pounding like drums, and the men go away.

You walk through the next night. You are hungry until you can steal some food from a farm near a town. You hide another night in a barn.

She talks often about hair, and the next day you both get it all cut off.

You hate the town, but you like the ferry, and then the train—the train best of all. The rattle and steam as you pull away. You both jig up and down, your hand holding her hand.

Ronan O'Driscoll

The Great Houdini

Lobby of the Palmer House Hotel, Monroe St., Chicago, IL. February, 1923.

Houdini: Please: have a seat. They really have done a fine job on the Palmer, haven't they? I very much like the new lobby. Coffee?

Charles B. Driscoll: Thank you, sir. Feels like…a palace. I expect you have stayed here many times down through the years.

Houdini: Oh, the odd time. I'm in Chicago a lot. S.A.M. has a big chapter here. Several spiritual con-artists have set up shop in this fine city. I'm delighted to hear you want to expose their activities.

Driscoll: Ah. That's the thing. Mr. Houdini, I'm not only reporting for my paper. I'm also doing a book about pirate treasure buried in the wilds of Eastern Canada. A place called Oak Island in Nova Scotia. Don't alarm yourself, sir. I'm looking into a medium, a Spiritualist called Anna Eva Fay. She visited there some years ago and claimed knowledge of Captain Kidd's treasure. Do you know her?

Houdini: [After a pause] Nova Scotia? Haven't been out there in a long time. I know Fay. She's a…competent performer. She let slip that she doesn't believe one whit in Spiritualism, Theosophy or whatever they're calling it these days. We discussed specifics of the trade and she says she can do it all: table levitation, fiddles that play themselves, seances. All the usual. I never met her in Nova Scotia, though. She performed there the year before I did. [Chuckles] She's making a big mistake going into specifics like buried treasure. Do you believe her?

Driscoll: No, no. Just a quote from you on the topic would be of considerable benefit. So many myths around this treasure have grown up out there. There's a stone with a cryptic message and a shaft deep beneath an island with several devious traps. Many have tried to excavate it and found nothing.

Houdini: Whole thing sounds like a con. Trust me, I know a fake when I hear one.

Driscoll: I'll…I'll keep that in mind. [Clears throat] Maybe we could talk about yourself? I'd also like to ask a few background questions about your famous acts. This is for the paper, you understand? For example, how did you come up with your famous strait-jacket escape?

Houdini: I might be out to expose frauds like Fay, but I won't be telling all my own secrets. [Laughs] I suppose I can tell you how I became captivated by straitjackets. Funny you mention the Maritimes. Near where your buried treasure lies, in Saint John, New Brunswick, was an insane asylum. *The Provincial Lunatic Asylum,* I think they called it. Terrible place. We did a performance there. Around '95 or '96, I believe. Let me see. I suppose it was really for charity. Although we were the ones in need of charity. The month before they ran us out of Halifax because our show's sponsor, Marco the Magician, had a name similar to some other conman called Markos. Also, Marco had a hypnotism act that went badly. Never try hypnotism, too many things can go wrong. To cap it all, Marco promised catching a bullet between the teeth but didn't. We had to escape out the back before being lynched. Tough audiences in that part of the world! [Pause] I'll never forget that asylum.

Terrible. Poor creatures. One kept rocking back and forth. Violent. They put him in a jacket. A straitjacket. Well, I had never seen one before that time. Although I had played the Wild Man in the circus. Again, it was the early days. So I suppose I felt sympathetic.

Driscoll: It became your signature act...

Houdini: Yes, you're right. But I saw something in that poor soul. Trapped in his own insanity. I felt trapped, too. No money or prospects. Wanted escape. It took some practice and hard work. These things do. I expect that might be why the strait-jacket escape became so popular. Everyone wants to escape.

Driscoll: Did you ever go back?

Houdini: To the Maritimes? No. I don't think I have. But when I finally made it—became successful, you know —I wrote to poor old Marco. His actual name was Dooley. Michael Dooley. Second generation Irish in Halifax. That part of the world is full of Irish. They hide, though. Anyway, I thanked him for the chance even though we went broke. I always felt that if I could wriggle out of that tight corner, I could do anything.

Driscoll: And the wild soul in the asylum?

Houdini: Him? Never got his name. Maybe he escaped, too. Out of that awful place and that cruel jacket. Who knows?

Pier 21

Halifax, October, 1929

Reverend Emmett Forrestall, the steel wall of the ship behind him, stepped down the gangway at the new liner terminal. He could not believe this was the same place he had left. Everything had changed into America from the movies; nothing was like the British backwater he remembered.

He caught a taxi, and gazed in amazement at the strange cars, department stores, and neon signs on Barrington Street. This was his first visit since his hasty departure from the North End Deepwater pier nearly forty years ago. At first he flinched at people looking at him as he walked by. *Do they recognize me?*

The year was 1929 and Halifax was booming, with no end in sight to the good times. All the ruin wreaked by the 1917 Explosion Emmett had read about was forgotten. There were new financial buildings and banks of ten or more storeys on Hollis Street and Bedford Row—Cheapside market long gone.

Emmett kept his pale face against the glass of his hotel room window, gazing down on it all. He felt like a phantom, trapped in an attic. He was staying at the Queen, down the street from the Halifax Club. That was still there. It surprised him how guilty he had felt walking past its snooty facade.

"Dddddrring! Dddddrrring!"

Emmett almost jumped out the window with fright.

"Dddddrring! Dddddrrring!"

The telephone, a malevolent black bakelite insect, made its insistent ring from his bedside table. He hated the things and refused to have one in his rectory.

He took a steadying sigh and walked over to pick up the handset.

"Reverend Forrestall?"

"Yes? Speaking."

"A local call for you, sir. A Reverend Merrick. Will I put him through?"

"Please."

Reverend Jonathan Merrick was the junior pastor at St. George's. He had telegraphed Emmett news of his mother's death. Emmett had to miss the funeral, airfare being an outrageous expense. It had taken nearly three weeks to get here.

"Jon Merrick here. Is that Emmett?"

The voice was polished. Emmett could sense the charisma over the electronic amplification.

"Ah, yes. How d'you do."

"Getting settled in all right?"

"Yes. Fine, thank you."

"Good." A pause. "Must be something, coming back after so long."

Emmett said nothing.

"Yes. Well, perhaps you'd like to pop over for a visit tomorrow? I can drive you over to Fairview, if you like."

Fairview? Didn't that used to be mostly farms?

"The cemetery. Where your mother's buried." Embarrassed laugh. "Oh, I expect that's since your time. Getting to be quite famous, actually. Many of the dead from the *Titanic* ended up there."

Emmett couldn't think what to say. "Thank you," he mumbled eventually.

"My pleasure. I'll call for you. Tomorrow at eleven."

~

Tall poplars and maples fringed the cemetery, their leaves starting to turn. Jonathan led Emmett down the hill to the corner where his mother was recently interred. He maintained a respectful distance while Emmett stood by the freshly-turned sod and pretended to pray.

The headstones all about were humble, no weeping angels or Doric columns.

After what Emmett judged enough time, he turned back towards the younger man.

"We considered it best for you to decide the wording of the headstone. The memorial quote and all that..." Jonathan cleared his throat delicately. "There is also the minor matter of the settling of her affairs..."

"Of course," Emmett said. "I tried to discuss that with father but...you know."

"How is the Reverend? The parish still speaks so fondly of him."

He's as demented as can be, Emmett thought. *He didn't know me from the orderly.* The old gent's home they put him in was ghastly. Not much better than the poor farm long ago. "He'll be delighted to hear that," he lied. "He's as well as can be expected, given..."

Emmett gestured at his mother's grave.

Jonathan gave a frowning nod. "How is your own wife? I'm sure you miss her terribly at this time..."

My wife? The one who hardly speaks to me? He wished this Merrick would leave him alone. Probably been told to keep an eye on him, in case Emmett absconded without paying.

"Harriet's well. She so wanted to visit Canada. Never been."

"Your mother spoke often of her. And your daughter."

"Really?" Had his mother gone senile, too? Before the end. Emmett wrote to her, but not regularly.

"Oh yes. She often boasted at our events of your accomplishments."

God. Who knew what fictions she created in his name. "I suppose we'd best be going," Emmett said to change the subject.

"Right. Back along this path. By the way, over there is Ernest King." Jonathan pointed towards a grave. "Purser on the *Titanic*, you know. Father was a Rector in Ireland. One of your lot, I'd say."

Emmett shook his head. Merrick spoke about religious denominations like football teams or corporations. He had even mentioned *"spiritual stocks and bonds"* on their drive. Might explain why he drove a shiny new Essex Coupe. Emmett couldn't imagine what the older parishioners made of him.

"Does it say where he's from?" Emmett said.

Jonathan shrugged, then strode off toward an arc of low headstones. Most bore numbers without names. One prominent one announced the Purser as a resident of Currin Rectory, Clones, Ireland.

"Clones?" Jonathan mispronounced. "Know it?"

"Yes. It's Clo-nes. Not far from us. County Monaghan."

"It's funny." Jonathan's grin was impressive. "You don't sound like you're from here. You sound very Irish, if you don't mind me saying."

Emmett smiled. *You have no idea what a compliment that is.*

Nowadays, Emmett only spoke in terse phrases, like the taciturn Londonderry farmers he served. An artist of silence, he perfected muteness and the avoidance of troublesome speech. His sermons were short, direct and appreciated by the parish he had lived in for the last twenty years.

The miracle of clear expression he had tried to force onto Stewart, he had successfully willed onto himself. Most people didn't even know.

The next day, Jonathan Merrick drove him out to the poor farm. Jonathan was surprised at Emmett's request, but accepted the explanation of the place being of "personal significance."

They sped along country roads, splashing through autumnal puddles. Emmett realized how much he preferred the Nova Scotia fall. The crisp air and myriad-coloured leaves were much preferable to the gloomy drizzle of autumn near Coleraine.

Merrick spoke incessantly: about the price he got his Essex for, investments he could recommend to Emmett, his own desire to move out, perhaps to Ontario. Emmett half-listened, distracted by how familiar the countryside became the further from Halifax they went.

"Wait. I think we passed it."

"Oops." Jonathan smiled, reversing the car on the narrow Bissett Road.

They regarded the weathered sign reading "County Farm". The gate was gone and the road choked with weeds.

"Are you sure you want us to go down there? I just washed the Essex."

"Oh, I'll walk down alone."

Merrick raised his eyebrows. "Alone? What if anything happens...?"

Emmett chuckled at the thought. "I'll be fine. Why don't you take a spin down to Cow Bay? Lovely spot."

Merrick gripped the steering wheel, his leather driving gloves making an irritated squeak. "But what am I to do down there?"

"Regard God's handiwork."

Leaving Emmett by the sign, a sour Merrick sped off toward the sea, having promised to return in an hour.

Tramping about the overgrown fields, Emmett found it hard to see exactly where the old buildings had been. Then he came upon them—a hell of blackened embers wet from the recent rain. He wandered about, reminded of the crumbling ruins of a famine village he visited once in Ireland, only this was fresher. *What had happened to everyone?*

Angela, his mother's housekeeper, had kept in touch, sending him letters with the occasional newspaper clipping. The Turners lasted a few more years as Matron and Keeper, despite accusations of book-keeping irregularities. Squire Bissett's political fortunes changed, and they were removed in 1899. James Turner died suddenly on the farm, leaving Eunice to manage alone without pay for several months. Destitute, she sued Council for her final wages.

Years later, his own mother mentioned the horrible fire at *"your poor farm"* in her last letter to him. No one knew the cause, but it spread quickly. They suspected the corridors between the buildings.

Emmett wondered what was to happen to the place now.

He picked his way through the charred ruins, remembering his visits here. There were more buildings than he remembered. They must have expanded in later years. He could ask Merrick for more details, but he didn't think he could bear to listen to him for much longer.

Was this the little room where he had conducted his 'experiments'?

What a fool I was!

He walked through bramble and among small trees, down towards the shore. The undergrowth was thick with blackberries, blackcurrants, haw and crab-apples. *Was that a quince bush?* He had forgotten those.

The water of the harbour was tranquil, just as he remembered it. He spotted the ruin of the Dead House past a large spruce. The roof had been tumbled and the stones scattered. There were low mounds in the rough ground all about. The unmarked graves.

They could have buried Stewart around here somewhere. If he died here. Had he kept singing? Had his genuine mother come for him?

And Sally McMahon? He wondered what had become of her. His mind filled with an image of her as old as himself, behind the counter of a tavern; Stewart helping her.

Standing on the shore, listening to the low hush of the sea, he realized they were his biggest mistake. Out of all the catalogue of errors in his life, a life spent describing and proscribing people's sins, why hadn't he helped them? Instead of scurrying away on a ship to Ireland, couldn't he have gone back to help?

Regret burned him as he wished to return to that callow youth he had been, back here to the poor farm, and warn them. Help them away from this terrible place. Help himself.

A shock of realization: he had abandoned his own self here, nearly forty years ago. His life since had been soulless: a hollow vessel going through the motions of living. Returning now, over sixty years of age, he had hoped to find something here. There was nothing, not even a ghost.

He turned away from the estuary and made his slow way up the hill to the road where the car would be waiting.

The Prindle

Dartmouth, Nova Scotia, present day

I blinked my eyes open. That didn't do it. I rubbed and poked at them to clear away the gumminess. *What the hell dream was that?* I remembered being told...something important. And running away. Finding happiness. It faded away as I focused on snatches of it.

Light crept at the edges of my room, and I wondered what time it might be. I felt around the bedside for my phone. 10:11. Good thing it was Saturday.

I slumped back down on the pillow. Never mind the dream, what else was I forgetting? *Something about today.* I rubbed the sandpaper stubble on my face, unable to recall.

My hand strayed to the other side of the bed. No one there. I found my glasses and sat up. A few tentative swallows. Mouth dry and bitter. Better check on Daniel.

Daniel!

Today was his day.

I pulled on clothes, making lots of noise to rouse him.

It was past eleven by the time the morning routine was out of the way and I could load him into the car. At least the mall was close. I had hoped to get him there by eleven to get acclimatized. It helped being the first ones there to familiarize. *Minimize surprises.*

I shook my head. He was playing a hip-hop playlist on his tablet in the back, and the lyrics were making my thoughts rhyme. He rarely stayed on one song for longer than five or ten seconds: always swiping through to the next, the music blaring through the car speakers. It was frustrating at first, but I'm used to it now.

I don't mind, really. His playing music on the tablet opened a world of communication. I hold his hand, and we tap out song titles. In his eagerness, he often calls out the next letter. *We never even knew he could read.* This lead to his using snatches of songs to converse, altering them as needed. "Baby, please don't go" became "Can I please don't go," meaning he wanted to go.

I reached behind me, palm extended. I received a light tap of acknowledgement. This was how we communicated. If I didn't get a replying tap, the faintest high-five, I would know something was up. I still try to get him to talk and engage, but this was often as good as it got.

Sometimes, driving, there were the exceptional times. One of us would hum a song and the other would echo it back, chortling at the other's version.

I once tried having him sit up front in the passenger seat, beside me. This worked fine at first. He would beam at me and jig back and forth in his seat, radio blaring. He was as happy as the times we sang together.

"Change it!" he insisted after a while.

"You're a big man now," I told him, nodding at the radio buttons. "You can change the music how you want."

Smiling, he pulled at the gear selector. The car shrieked as he threw us into reverse. I cursed while the car stalled. The truck behind us screeched, avoiding a collision but blaring their horn in anger.

I had to swear my way back into drive and pull the car over, nodding appeasingly at the furious truck driver.

After a few deep breaths, I calmed down and coaxed him into the back seat. He sullenly kept asking to "change it" for the rest of the journey. No more sitting up front.

Later, he figured out the tablet. I hooked it up over Bluetooth so he could play whatever he wanted, scrolling through as if he were driving the music.

I glanced down at the gear selector. *Gear stick?* What was the proper name here? My Canadian father-in-law jokingly called it the Prindle. When I arrived first, he taught me how to drive on the other side with an automatic. P-R-N-D-1-2-3. Prindle. As good a name as any. The word sounded like an important part of an antique agricultural machine, something farmers might have cursed and puzzled over.

"Y'all right there, Daniel?" I asked as we drove down our street.

No reply.

"Nervous at all?"

His only response was to swipe to 'Fight the power'. I stopped glancing at him in the rear-view mirror and focused on turning onto the main road.

The morning was quiet. Few cars about. Stopped at a traffic light, my thoughts idled on where to park at the mall. The old Walmart entrance was probably the best. I pondered stopping at the Tims before remembering we were running late. For an audition.

This is crazy.

I would never have gone for it except for his music therapist. In the last year, he amazed everyone with his ability to sing certain songs from memory. The songs he picked seemed random, from diverse genres: Rock, Pop, Rap. Country songs were the toughest to put up with. He occasionally mispronounced words, giving the game away. He was parroting the sounds. It was hard to know what the songs meant to him, if they meant anything.

As I merged onto the highway, a sudden panic overtook me. How would he do? Would they jeer at his weird antics? Would he refuse to go, have a meltdown right in front of everyone?

I eyed the bulk of the shopping mall looming beyond the next exit, MIC MAC MALL emblazoned in giant letters on a sign. I did a double take when I saw it the first time. Was it meant to be Irish? Some kind of twist on "Knick Knack Paddywhack"?

I later discovered it was a kind of slur, but for the Mi'kmaq.

Predictably, traffic was busier closer to the mall. It was always jammed on a Saturday. What if a shooter showed up and put the whole place on lockdown?

This had almost happened a number of years ago, at another Halifax mall. Some young woman from Illinois convinced a couple of locals to grab guns and go shoot up the mall on Valentine's Day. They were caught before it got out of hand, but didn't that kind of thing lead to copycat attempts? If it happened, at least it meant we wouldn't have to appear on stage.

I negotiated the car into a parking spot, reflecting on what kind of memorial they might put up for the slain. There were plenty of empty spots in the failing mall where they could erect a mural: a listing of names with a depiction of something stark, like a row of crosses. Perhaps they would have actual crosses, depending on the scale of the massacre.

"Let's go, big man. Time to face the music."

He unhooked his seat belt and got out of the car. He was humming something, almost under his breath. I didn't quite catch it, but it could have been 'Three Little Birds' by Bob Marley.

"Don't think you want to sing that one. Remember the one we practised."

He said nothing. I shoved his tablet into a backpack and we walked toward the mall entrance.

On one of the glass doors was a small printed sign with a multi-coloured logo:

**Canada Can Sing!
Auditions Upper Atrium**

Oh, god. Were we really doing this?

I looked back at him, walking behind me in his usual disconnected way. It would be easy to head over to the food court, get something from one of the fast-food chains and then head home. Maybe go on a walk somewhere. Escape...

Remember that time as a teenager when you ran away from a disco in Ennis? *The Outer Limits*. That was the name of the place. You were supposed to meet your cousins inside. You had even paid the cover and wandered in. Mirrors, nicotine fug, and girls dancing around their handbags. There was even someone wearing wellington boots. Ennis was a more rural town then.

And you ran. Face burning with embarrassment, you hurried out against the incoming crowd. Out into the cool drizzle. All night you wandered the quiet streets. You stopped by the river Fergus, staring into the black water. *Why?* Why had such a panic come over you? *What the hell was wrong with me?*

It wasn't the rustic nightclub as much as...the noise. Whatever current racket was belting out over the speakers had acted as a force field—repelling you. *Odd.* It never made sense before.

You studied Daniel as both of you rose up in the elevator, multiple versions of each other reflected in the mirrored walls.

"I suppose we're not that different."

After a few hours of roaming about the quiet town, you had ended up at your aunt's place and slipped into the house. Your cousins joined after a while. No one mentioned your disappearance. What was that? Thirty years ago? Ancient history.

"Hi! Are you here to audition?"

The woman at the entrance to the atrium wore bright makeup. A professional mask. Warpaint. It must be handy to disguise yourself like that.

An awkward pause. You could still escape.

"Ah. Yes. We are. I mean, he is. In the young adult category."

"Great! Want to sign in there, bud?"

"No," Daniel murmured, looking at the ground.

I laughed, speaking quickly to cover my embarrassment. "'Course he does. He's just a bit nervous."

Her smile was magnanimous and patronizing.

I quickly filled in our names on the forms, waivers and so on. She filled in an ID card with his name on it, attached it to a lanyard and held it out. Daniel took it without a word.

"Awesome," she said, without enthusiasm. "Can't wait to hear you sing, Daniel."

More uncomfortable silence.

"Ah, um," I flustered. "He's autistic. Doesn't speak much."

"Doesn't speak?" she repeated, a laugh in her voice. "How's he going to sing?"

I reddened with shame. This really was a terrible idea. The other kids in the line behind us were giggling and looking at one another.

I saw myself exploding: screaming at her with all my frustration and doubt, pulling him out of there past all the judging gazes.

Instead, I took a deep breath, swallowed and nodded. "Thank you," I said, voice too bright. "Come on, Daniel. Let's go take our place."

Her exquisite eyebrows arched even more as we walked past, Daniel holding my hand. I thought I heard murmured amazement from the teenagers behind us.

The TV production company had cordoned off most of the upper section of the mall. Half of the folding chairs were empty, the other half a motley selection of parents, sharply-attired contestants and bored onlookers.

Daniel had a black shirt on, speckled with stylized comets, stars and nebulae. I had resisted this choice but it suited him. He looked deceptively older, a capable young man.

The stage was a spotlit area at the far end of the atrium, festooned with cables and large speakers. A pair of young black men made very slick sounds on keyboards. The good-looking one sang beautifully, eyes closed. The judges said little, taking notes on clipboards, their table only a few metres away.

When the young men finished, the handsome lead singer looked at the judges with expectation.

"Thank you, Beales Brothers." the judge on the left, a thin-lipped woman in black, said. "Next, please."

The next few acts were all different but shared amateur mediocrity. A few times, I thought Daniel might get up and leave. He remained focused, even jiggling his hands in time to some of the music. Still, I kept a tub of yellow Play-doh ready in case he needed distraction.

A skinny youth in goth makeup and spiked hair took the mic. He started singing a capella but halted after a few lines as his act fell apart. He kept stumbling on the same word, staring in terror at the snickering crowd.

Unable to take any more, he ran off the stage area, black tears staining his whitened face.

"Thank you, Majesterio," the judge said, deadpan. "Next, please."

Horrified, I realized that was us. The pit of my stomach lurched.

"Daniel," I whispered. "It's okay. We should go. This was a bad idea."

I could see the woman who greeted us at the entrance, tilting her head in sarcastic inquiry. She was waiting for us to bolt.

"You go," he said.

I understood "you go" as "I go". I breathed a heavy sigh of relief, mind jumping to what steps to take to escape with the least damage. I was glad he understood. The right thing to do was to get out of here as quick as we could. Plus, we could say we tried.

Daniel stood and walked up to the stage. Mouth agape, I watched him step up to the microphone. He held onto the mic and made a small smile right to me. He looked re-laxed as any natural—singing to crowds all his life.

The crowd, and my panic about them, vanished like ghosts from one hundred years ago. *How?* was all my mind could register as I watched him lean into the micro-phone's black foam and begin

to sing

THE END

Acknowledgements

I would like to thank the Cole Harbour Heritage Museum for their wonderful local history archives. Curator Heather Adams introduced me to Nancy Muzzatti's unpublished historical report on the Cole Harbour Poor Farm. Thank you, Nancy, for your excellent research and assistance. It was key to my understanding of the real people who lived on the poor farm. Thanks also for background on the gravesite to Terry Eyland, manager of the Dartmouth Heritage Museum. Of course, any historical mistakes are my own.

The songs quoted in *Poor Farm* are thanks to Helen Creighton, the collector of Maritime folk songs. She was as key to preservation of the traditional music of this province as Francis O'Neill was to Irish music. Thanks to Clary Croft for introducing me to her work.

Being a parent of someone on the spectrum has helped make me a better person. I have learned so much from my amazing (but often mischievous!) son, Martin. It also helps to have a great support network. There are too many to mention here but I would like to single out the other parents and staff of PLT (Playing and Learning Together), the non-profit autism after-school program where I am lucky enough to serve on the board. Thanks, guys! I am constantly amazed by your talent and dedication to our kids.

I'd like to thank my fellow writers at the Bedford Writers Group for putting up with my rough drafts. Special thanks to our group founder, Suzanne Atkinson.

Thanks for reading the whole thing twice and setting me right, Suzanne. I would also like to thank Jane Simpson and Gerard Collins of the "Go and Write!" retreat. Gerard is an exceptional mentor and friend. Thanks also to Niki Davison of Snickerdoodle photography for the photos and writing advice. Special mention to Marilyn Smulders of the Writer's Federation of Nova Scotia. We've come a long way from CQ5, Marilyn!

Finally, I would like to thank Moose House Publications for taking a chance on me. Brenda Thompson and Andrew Wetmore (despite his love of the Oxford Comma!) are incredible to work with. This book owes a lot to their dedication and innovative approach to publishing rural Nova Scotia stories. I am honoured to be a part of it.

About the author

Originally from the West of Ireland, Ronan O'Driscoll lived in Chicago, Dublin and Japan before settling in Dartmouth, Nova Scotia with his wife and children. A software developer and educator, he has always enjoyed writing. His first novel, *Chief O'Neill*, pays homage to his love of history and traditional Irish music.

His casual discovery of unmarked graves from a 19th-century "Poor Farm for the Harmlessly Insane" in Cole Harbour sparked his interest and research for this book.

9 781777 293789